July 2005

— for U, (my beautiful Raymond)
L + L + L !
q
Jack is dear to my
heart — hope you'll
enjoy his writing —

MEMOIRS OF A MOTH

Jack Chalfin

authorHOUSE™

1663 LIBERTY DRIVE, SUITE 200
BLOOMINGTON, INDIANA 47403
(800) 839-8640
WWW.AUTHORHOUSE.COM

© 2005 Jack Chalfin. All Rights Reserved.

First published by AuthorHouse 06/08/05

ISBN: 1-4208-4833-X (sc)

Printed in the United States of America
Bloomington, Indiana

This book is printed on acid-free paper.

For Claire and Max, as always

Chapter 1

If I'm not who I say I am, you'll forgive me. Sometimes the best way to view yourself is through a frosted glass, and if I tell this story the way it *should* have been, it's not from a desire to deceive, but only from the need to take a step away from the pain. That means taking two steps away from reality. With rounded edges and, most of all, the possibility of hope, the essence of the story is the same. This is my memoir. I am the Moth.

The tale begins with a painting. Leo Schultz, tallish, thinnish, broodingly handsome– an obscure painter until *Schoolbuses* was first shown and sold in a bidding war for twice the original asking price. Then, everything changed.

I know everything there is to know about Leo– his innermost thoughts, his emotions, how oil paints smell to him when he first squeezes them from the tube, even the way Dara's silky skin feels against his own. It's a secret more than a talent.

Just back from his obligatory two years in Paris, Leo was living in New York and experimenting with different styles of painting, trying to find one that suited him. The man could paint, it was just a question of how? If only the right *how* would come to him, the *what* was sure to follow.

Finding what to paint wasn't a new problem. Leo never connected to his work. Though precociously talented, he lost interest in every piece as soon as the paint had dried on the canvas. The young artist hadn't yet accomplished a painting that had been extruded from his soul. Before passion and vision would come, he needed discipline and technique. So for two years in Paris, while waiting for the passion, he honed his skills of color and shapes and values and perspective and composition. To save money, he painted over most of the canvases four and five times until the surface was too soft from layers of paint to use again. Everything was an exercise, nothing worth saving– although in later years, the University auctioned off some of his "early works" that were really just soggy throwaways.

Ambitious, but without prospect, Leo moved back to New York without experiencing Paris in any real sense– and without so much as a beret– and rented a small apartment in the East Village.

The apartment was perfect for an intense young artist. Cheap and sunlit, it suited him, even though the neighborhood was decaying rapidly. The living room had high windows facing south, so there was good light during most of the day, but he painted at all hours and would have used lit matches to illuminate his easel if necessary.

Those early days, the habits and traits he developed as a young man, round out the image of the older Leo who came into my life when I needed him so much.

Manhattan, in the sixties, was bubbling with artists creating Art that ranged from classical motifs to the most avant garde– paintings that were neither *paintings*, nor necessarily *Art*. Leo looked at them all– from hotel lobbies and bookstore walls to the major galleries and museums– then went back to his studio to try to capture their spirit for his own. Nothing took hold until his muse stood to attention at an exhibit by Richard Estes.

Photorealism was not considered *pure* enough for the true artist until the late sixties, and Leo had never tried painting in that style during his schooling. The exactitude of the form appealed to Leo's technical side, and was an excellent test of the skills he had hoped to master in Paris. At least it was an idea, and gave him something new to paint. Leo bought an old Leica from a pawnshop and walked around the city for weeks taking pictures.

Of all the pictures he took, there were two that stood out. One was taken from the fourth floor of a building looking down at a swarming crowd of people trying to cross Fifth Avenue and 46th Street at the end of a work day. The photograph overflowed with energy and the juxtaposition of the geometric streets and buildings offset by the undisciplined, swarming crowd produced a compelling visual image. The other picture showed an old, empty school bus parked on the side of a rain-swept street in Tribeca. The colors and textures were so overpowering that they were almost palpable.

Schoolbuses was born from those two shots. The painting began as another exercise, but by the third day, became his mission. Leo worked almost nonstop for two weeks until it was finished. His life was never the same. My life was never the same.

Leo tells my story as if it was his own.

Chapter 2

Buses showed at Richard "Mo" Morrison's gallery. Mo became my advisor and my friend throughout my life, and I owe him much. Our relationship wasn't unflawed, though. For instance, it was at one of Mo's openings where I first met Sylvie. She was smart and beautiful, and had a master's degree in art history. Sylvie worked as an assistant at Bruno Graham's gallery down the street, and aspired to be an art critic. Those facts about Sylvie all came later. Our first encounter occurred when she walked into Mo's gallery– a simple act, which produced an immediate visceral rush within me. I hadn't been with a woman for a long time. Certainly not in Paris, and since my return to New York, I'd been immersed in my painting. There had been little time for even thoughts about sex.

The sight of Sylvie poured over me in a way that was beyond rational control. There had been several girlfriends in college to whom I was emotionally attached in varying degrees, but I'd never had such a completely physical and mindless response to any of them. Here was a woman who was a complete stranger, yet for whom I was willing to trade my soul. As it turns out, I did.

Moving by the dictates of her own agenda as she always did, Sylvie was already making her way toward me. When she came

4

up behind me and touched my elbow, her touch triggered a bolt of lightning that sped down my spine. As it passed, I turned and smelled Sylvie for the first time. Her smell had an other-worldliness– it was a place more than a smell. A place I wanted to be.

The smell amplified my lust, making my body ache. She was pretty, but there were dozens of equally beautiful women in the room. Sylvie radiated an aura that bonded to mine on a molecular level.

She introduced herself and said all those self-deprecating, *I'm in the presence of a genius* things you're supposed to say. There wasn't the time to waste on inanities. I couldn't go through all the niceties and coyness of a prolonged seduction, nor even wait a second longer. Breathing her in was not enough.

We left the gallery and went to bed.

The sex, as predictable after all those years of preoccupied celibacy, was fantastic, and I was a goner, right away. During the weeks that followed, Sylvie did nothing to break the spell. On the contrary, she became more and more attractive to me. Besides the sex, she was smart and knowledgeable about art. In those early days, it didn't seem that she was holding me at arms' length, that I was a specimen more than a lover. Not that it mattered. Not then. And there was always the lingering smell of Sylvie on my clothes, my body, my mind.

We were married in a very small wedding the night after the opening of my second show at Mo's. Sylvie's father was there, as was my brother Zach, and Mo and Barbara. My parents had died within months of each other, just before my triumphant first show, never getting to see the fruit of their belief in me. I wasn't struck by the oddity that the bride had no friends to invite. We moved into

Sylvie's place on the Upper East Side, but I kept my East Village apartment as a studio.

Sylvie's plan for herself included marriage and fame. Now that we were married, she focused on recreating her persona and becoming famous while I lapsed back into my old work habits. Soon after the wedding, we were living very disparate lives. My new bride trotted me out at important social events as her prize celebrity husband and media magnet– my second show was even better received than the first– but otherwise had little use for me. Another man might have been upset by what we had become. Not Leo Schultz. I was too caught up in my own world to notice.

We missed the whole newlyweds-developing-intimacy-and-a-shared-life routine because we spent so little time together, and when we did, we interacted more like casual friends than like newlyweds and lovers. Now that we were married, the sex tapered rapidly. Sylvie kept me at bay, only growing warmer when she needed me to appear somewhere with her. A mere stepping stone to Sylvie's loftier goals, my personal usefulness was over– superfluous and threatened, like a male Black Widow spider in the aftermath of the mating ritual.

Three months after the wedding, I had my first fugue in almost ten years. Fugue states were part of my life ever since I was three years old. They came at irregular intervals, sometimes with many years between them, and lasted from hours to weeks– although most of them were several days long. Amazingly, through all those years, they never came at a time, or in a way that endangered me. Suddenly, I felt very tired, and then it would be days later. To others, I appeared to be in a deep and unarousable sleep, while I experienced darkness with some subtle swirling lights and absolute silence. When it was over, there was a seamless transition back to wakefulness, leaving me totally refreshed and in an expansive mood.

My parents, of course, panicked the first time it happened, and it happened several times during that first year. No abnormality was ever discovered, even years later when medical technology caught up to my affliction. The child psychiatrists and psychologists stepped in to offer various learned theories, but no two of them ever quite agreed, and everyone eventually stopped paying attention to them.

The maybe-imminent fugues were always a lurking presence in our family although Zach, who was born after they started, regarded them as just one more facet of his life. Some guys had brothers who were good baseball players, Zach had a brother who had fugues. Dara says that the stigma of the fugues is what made me so withdrawn from other people. Gwen needs the fugues to explain my absences. Zach maintains that I was just born surly.

Despite the six-year age difference between my brother Zach and me, we were together a lot when we were young. Zach is very smart and always seemed older than his age. He became a chemist and works for a pharmaceutical conglomerate in New Jersey, where he lives. Although I still feel very close to Zach, his wife, and his two sons, we hardly ever see one another, and maintain contact with sporadic phone conversations and at infrequent family occasions.

My childhood fugues were nothing more than sustained time outs. The one that occurred right after my marriage to Sylvie was very different, but became the blueprint for all those that followed. Besides being revitalized and happy, I came out of the fugue no longer intrigued with photorealism, and consumed with the need to do abstract expressionism.

The repercussions of abandoning the technique that had made me rich and famous were not lost on me. My improbable success

7

afforded me with a promising future, allowing me to do exactly what I wanted to do. Could I possibly switch genres— a pretentious word I never like to use— and not commit professional suicide? The question was obvious and rational, but it didn't matter. There simply was no choice. Mo almost swallowed his telephone when he heard the news. When he finally collected himself, he solicited Sylvie's aid to persuade me, or badger me if necessary, to reconsider the change.

The "discussion" that night with Sylvie, was the first of, alas, many venomous, vituperative, meanspirited, self-absorbed fights we had on a regular basis until, and for sometime after, the ultimate dissolution of our wedded bliss. During the first argument, I was little more than a spectator, but later rose to the task with each succeeding fight, and was just as meanspirited as Sylvie before it was all over.

My beloved wife had been oblivious to my recent six-day fugue, which I had been considerate enough to conduct at my studio. Her indifference to my absence was one more sign of the ever-growing trouble in our marriage, and one which even I could no longer ignore.

Sylvie's attack was unipolar. She had hitched her star to my worthless, marginally talented, misanthropic, sex-crazed, obsessed, pathetic little soul, and I wasn't keeping my part of the bargain. There was no way she'd let me throw away her future and all she had worked towards, on a whim.

Mo was kinder and more circumspect, but equally unnerved and alarmed. He understood, he told me, about genius–blah, blah, blah– and Muses– blah, blah, blah– and the artistic temperament– blah, blah, blah– but he felt obligated to say something. He would be remiss, both professionally and as a friend, if he didn't warn me that I was using bad judgment.

This double pronged attack from Sylvie and Mo was a formidable alliance and, intellectually, I couldn't argue with their logic. But it still came back to one thing: I had no choice. There was no more inspired photorealism in me. I was already emotionally committed to the shapes and colors of a different style.

Mo barely looked at my first new painting, said nothing, and left quickly. But when he returned to review it alongside the second one, his face lit up and he muttered, *this could happen.* Eight paintings later, I was ready for a show– the only show I've ever done that I considered doing somewhere other than at Mo's because he kept insisting that he would also hang some of my photorealism– to be borrowed back from buyers because they had all been sold.

The critics were cynical as soon as word of the show leaked out, judging the new paintings before the paint was dry on the canvasses. They arrived at the preview with rough drafts of their scathing critiques already in their pockets, prepared to hate all of it. But they were surprised. The paintings were richly colored and textured, and were intended to be visually multilayered with unplumbed depths that promised additional surprises every time you looked. The images invited you to crawl in and wrap them around yourself. These ill-tempered art snobs liked my new work despite their better, and preformed, professional judgment. Mo beamed.

Sylvie, on the other hand, refused to attend the opening, nor ever deigned to look at the new work. Despite their critical success and the almost immediate sellout at outrageous prices, she never conceded that I had done the right thing by following my instincts. Her self-absorption and mawkishness stood in the way of her greed and her need to bask in my fame. She maintained her hostility toward me to the end. More than that, her stubborn unwillingness to alter her stance, marked our end.

Our relationship spiraled downward. Sylvie left her job at the Bruno Gallery to become the assistant to David Vandeross, the fine arts' critic for the prestigious *New York Review.* Mr. Vandeross was a mean, nit-picking son-of-a-bitch when he wasn't drinking, and a lot worse when he was in his usual state of controlled insobriety. He was the perfect preceptor for Sylvie– haughty, self-aggrandizing and an egomaniac. Sylvie's job consisted mainly of getting him his coffee and waiting, like all her disappointed predecessors, for his retirement. David Vandeross was not about to cede the power that his column gave him, but was not above stringing his assistants along for whatever benefits he might accrue from their fawning expectations. Although he always found my work *charming,* his reviews were tepid in comparison to the other critics.

Sylvie delighted in the reflected power of her new position, and vigorously used it to maximize her own cachet. Whether or not she was actually sleeping with her boss was the subject of much conjecture in the art world, but sex with the boss was generally considered to be part of the job description. She certainly wasn't sleeping with me. The woman who had once been the center of my ardor got harder and meaner, becoming almost dangerous. Soon, even her smell, now tainted by a whiff of her rotting core and a soupçon of flop sweat (her career had stagnated), no longer affected me.

Much against my protests, and in a move almost unheard of in those times, Mo had convinced me to have Sylvie sign a prenuptial agreement. The prenup turned out to be both a good thing – the marriage was dead, and she was a greedy, conniving little bitch– and a bad thing– it was economically more beneficial for her to stay married to me. We settled into our separate lives, both becoming uglier and uglier toward one another.

My paintings reflected the turmoil in my life. They were dark and convoluted, ready to explode. Mo couldn't get enough of them to satisfy the demand. My professional life flowered as my personal life deteriorated. We continued like that for almost three years until Sylvie met Mr. Right and, finally, wanted out.

By the time the divorce was final, even the passion of our hatred had been spent. We parted with incurable wounds and acrimony, but on better terms than we'd had through most of our marriage.

The relief to paint without the nagging interruption of Sylvie and her relentless annoyances had a tremendous effect on my work. The enraged energy of the last few years was nothing compared to the exuberance of my liberation. This self-contained pattern of obsessive and prolific painting continued for several more years until my next fugue.

I became a still-life painter.

Chapter 3

After three or four fugues with the accompanying changes in my painting style, Mo stopped panicking each time. The switches were done with accompanying bursts of enthusiasm that were communicated in my work, and the successes continued to flow as my riches grew. By now, my canvasses were in the permanent collections of most major, and a bunch of minor, museums, often representing more than one technique. I was the darling of the rich collectors– it became fashionable to own one of each of my types of painting. The body of my work included cubism, impressionism, surrealism, post-impressionism, and something the Dadaists liked to call dadaism. Each change was a dazzling success. For instance, during my portrait phase, almost every prominent New Yorker sat for me.

As fulfilled as I was as an artist, my personal life was stagnant and dismal. Mo and Barbara were my only contacts with the outside world. Ideas flowed from an inexhaustible reservoir, and my total involvement with my work left no time for anything else. I attended fewer and fewer openings, earning the deserved reputation of a recluse. Painting was everything, and all I wanted to do was paint.

The media described me as frenzied and possessed. Fortunately, the aura of eccentricity increased my stature in the art world.

Barbara occasionally invited me to a dinner or cocktail party in order to introduce me to women. I demurred. Not that I wasn't interested in women, it was just that my energy was all directed toward my painting.

So I painted.

And painted.

A dozen more years passed until just after my fortieth birthday. My canvasses had grown much larger and very detailed, and it took much longer to finish each one. Mo encouraged me to do a retrospective because too much time had elapsed since my last show, and there weren't enough completed works for a new one. The preparation for the retrospective was both hard work and emotionally draining. I had never shown or sold a painting that didn't mean a lot to me, so I had an emotional attachment to each of them. The effect was like seeing your children again after many years, and realizing how much you'd missed them.

The impact of the show was enormous and turned me into a lesser pop icon, culminating with my picture on the cover of *Time Magazine*. The people at *Time* treated me like royalty, and the photographers tried to show me at my best. But when I saw the cover, I was struck by the hollow, lost and semi-maniacal –I'm giving myself the benefit of the doubt here on the **semimaniacal**– look in my eyes, and the haggard look of my face despite their liberal use of the airbrush. Mo pressed me to take a vacation. The thought of going somewhere and not painting held no appeal for me. I compromised by working only in the morning, leaving me time to relax and reenter the world during the rest of the day.

That meant staying away from museums and art exhibits and going to a lot of movies and Off-Broadway plays. In between, I roamed the city, walking miles at a time to refresh my sense of New York. An attractive woman approached me during intermission one night outside a theater in The Village.

"Excuse me, I'm pretty sure you're Leo Shultz. I hope I'm not imposing, but I've wanted to meet you for some time. I'm Dara Harrington." She extended her hand.

"Not at all. I'm just waiting for the second act to begin." We shook.

"I work at Linstrom and Howes. We did the advertising for your retrospective."

"Did you have anything to do with the brochure?"

"That's why I recognized you. I did the cover and most of the layouts."

"Mo Morrison has the cover framed on his office wall. The design was inspired."

"Well, thank you. I won't take up any more of your time. I just wanted to say hello."

"Nice to meet you." Since the *Time* cover, I had been approached by strangers more than once.

She turned and left, then returned after a few steps.

"At the risk of sounding like a groupie, I'm here with two friends and, if you're free, we'd like you to join us for something to eat after the play."

There was something commanding about her gaze, the way she maintained eye contact and really looked at me. Her eyes were mesmerizing; beautiful and haunting at the same time. It would take a whole pallette of colors to paint those eyes. She seemed reserved, but more from politeness than shyness, and she carried herself with easy self-confidence. I agreed before I had time to think about it.

The other two women were equally attractive and had that savvy New York air that I like. One was the executive secretary to the president of an expensive watch company. The other was in middle management at the New York Hilton. The executive secretary, Ellen, was the talker and dominated the conversation, but she was witty and interesting. Much to everyone's surprise, the evening went well.

If painting *Schoolbuses* was a moment in time from which the rest of my life flowed, that evening at the theater was equally as important. Not only did I meet Ellen and Dara that night, but the intersection of my life with Gwen's became a possibility.

Pat, the Hilton executive, had no idea who I was (imagine!) while Dara was a fan and had been to all my shows since returning to New York in 1978. After dinner, we shared a cab home. Although I lived the closest, I insisted– out of some misguided macho sense of chivalry, I suppose– that I was the last one let off. Ellen remained next to last. When we got to her apartment, she invited me up, and when I begged off, she pressed her card in my hand.

Two days later, Ellen called me, leaving a message on my answering machine, which I leave on while painting. Though the noise of the incoming messages is almost as distracting as answering the phone, I didn't have to put down my brush to answer. No one ever called me who couldn't wait, and I never interrupted my work to pick up the phone. Few people ever called at all.

Ellen phoned five or six times that morning. This was supposed to be a vacation, so at one thirty, I forced myself to stop painting and returned her calls. She had an unexpected– it was contrived– day off and wondered if I would meet her for lunch. With no particular plans for the afternoon, I agreed.

Ellen was articulate and interesting– quite pretty with a body women twenty years younger would covet. She was also a woman on a mission. Me. Ellen turned on her charm. Other than occasional short and unfulfilling liaisons over the years since Sylvie, there had been no women in my life, so Ellen's success was all but guaranteed. She could have relaxed. I was ready to succumb to her wiles before we were passed the menus. When lunch was over and she asked if she could see my studio, I relaxed too– the possibility that I was misreading her signals had occurred to me.

Neither of us was disappointed that day. Ellen was an aggressive and imaginative lover, and everything clicked between us. Even after we were both exhausted and, for that day, done with sex, she was a great companion. Unlike Sylvie who, despite her acrobatics and intensity, always kept that slight coolness, Ellen held nothing back. She was, mind and body, all there and her unedited openness was new for me– much more satisfying and it felt good. By the end of that one day, I felt closer to Ellen than I had with any woman for quite some time.

Soon after we met, I gave up the pretense of vacation and went back to painting full tilt. Despite my all absorbing work pattern, we spoke on the phone once during the week, and Ellen came over late on Saturday nights. I didn't paint on Sundays so that we could spend the day together. If not exactly in love, we became great friends and were very comfortable with one another. Definitely a couple.

Six months later, I was ready for another show. As usual, the planning took several months to accomplish. During one of the interminable meetings we had in Mo's office, I found my eyes repeatedly drawn to Dara's cover.

"Mo, can you arrange to have Dara Harrington do the brochure for this show?"

"Dara's agency is doing the publicity for the show and she's a senior member of the team, so it's likely she'll be involved. I'll make the specific request, if you want."

"Well, make sure she's invited to the opening, in any case."

Whatever Mo was thinking, he suppressed a comment.

Ellen and I had never discussed Dara. Now, because I found myself thinking about her a lot, I wanted to know more about her. The impact of her eyes was still as intense as when I had first, and only, seen them months before. Ellen didn't have much to say. She only knew Dara through Pat, and hadn't spoken to Dara since the night we'd all been together; they weren't friends on their own. She knew that Dara was a single mother with a young daughter, and that Pat had said that she kept to herself a lot. Why?

I told her about the cover Dara had done for the retrospective, that she was very talented, and that I hoped she would do something equally as good for the new show. We dropped the subject.

When you consider that I'm a successful painter, it's no surprise that the two most important women in my life first come on stage at art shows. Dara was at the new opening, standing alone looking at one of my paintings. When Sylvie first walked into Mo's, I sensed her with my nose, the most primitive sense a human has. My reaction to Sylvie, my entire life with Sylvie, was primitive in all its aspects. Hormonal sex and feral fights. Dara reached me through my sight, the highest order of sensation, and the most important pathway to an artist's brain. She was bathed, not in the glow of desire, but in the aura of destiny. I grabbed two glasses of champagne from a passing waiter.

"Thanks, this is a treat. I mean all this," she said, gesturing around the gallery. "I've never been to an opening at a major gallery."

"That's strange. You know so much about art."

She narrowed her eyes while considering her response, visibly rejecting several possibilities before she spoke.

"We travel in different circles."

"Well, you seemed so familiar with my work. I felt guilty that I never invited you before."

"But we've only just met."

"True. But now that you're here, what do you think?"

"About the opening or about your paintings?"

"I'm an insecure painter obsessed with my own work. Which do you think I mean?"

She didn't hesitate at all. "These paintings are on a much larger scale than you've done before. They're like quicksand. You start to look and, suddenly, you're sucked in until you feel like you can't breathe. But good, not bad. Then the explosion of color sends you hurtling safely out of the quicksand with all your senses tingling. I don't want to ever stop looking."

"Wow, would you mind writing the reviews?"

We laughed and drank our champagne, then walked around together looking at the other pieces. Her comments were not only flattering, but almost frightening because of her insight into my thoughts about each one.

"Are you here with anyone?"

"I almost brought Gwen, my daughter, but she's only eleven and she would have been bored and unhappy. I haven't seen Ellen. Is she here?"

"No, she had to go to a sales conference in St. Martin this weekend. You know about us?"

"Pat told me you two have been dating since that night at the theater."

"I guess I have you to thank for bringing us together."

"More like serendipity. I wouldn't have planned it that way." Before I had time to consider what she meant, she changed the subject. "Do you keep any of your paintings?"

"I never have. If I kept one, I'd have to keep them all. Picking just one to keep would be impossible."

"Well, I know which one I would pick."

"Let me guess, either *Schoolbuses* or *Distressed Nude.*" These were the two most famous and both appeared in numerous collections and books. I was making an unfounded assumption about Dara– she already had shown a deeper grasp of my work than most people.

"No. Remember, I only get to have one, and I'm going to live with it forever, so it has to affect me in a personal way. I'd want *Junction.*" *Junction* was from my tumultuous and dark cusp-of-Sylvie period. An emotional cast of my psyche placed on canvas.

"Although, if I had a large enough room, I might take *Jasmine* from this show. I can't believe how you did such a large piece in pretty much all greens, and gave it such force and energy. And beauty"

"I wasn't sure I could pull it off, but that's why I did it. Do you paint?"

"No. I'm just a fan."

"You should. You draw so well, and you seem to understand the process of painting so intimately. At least my painting."

"My Uncle Jess, who was a podiatrist, used to come for dinner every Thanksgiving, and he was always given the job of carving the turkey. Uncle Jess carved it as well as anyone else ever does, but every year, my father ragged him about how he was a surgeon and couldn't even carve a turkey. As if one skill automatically transferred to the other. I feel the same way about graphic design and fine art. Not the same."

We had another glass of champagne.

"I have to go circulate a little, but everyone should be leaving soon. Can you stay a while longer? I want you to meet Mo."

"Sure, I'll see you later."

A lot more than a little later, when I was finally done schmoozing with prospective buyers, Dara had left.

Mo and Barbara and I held our postmortem in Mo's office. Mo was triumphant. The critics had all congratulated him and three paintings had already sold. These were, as I have said, huge canvasses and commanded a hefty price.

"Has *Jasmine* sold yet?" I asked, surprising myself with the impulsive leap I was about to take.

Mo consulted his notes. "No, not yet."

"Don't sell it. I'm going to keep it."

"What?"

"I said that I'm going to keep it. Call it a whim."

"A six figure whim!"

"Neither one of us needs any more money, Mo."

"You don't have two kids in school and a wife with a diamond habit." Barbara held up her bejeweled hands to demonstrate his point.

"Still. I don't want to sell it yet. Maybe later."

"It's your painting."

"For now."

My decision was pure caprice. Dara's comments had made me think. *Jasmine* was special to me because, even after years of being able to put whatever came into my head on canvas, when I conceived *Jasmine* I wasn't sure I could make it work. Also, after almost fifteen years of prolific painting, I didn't have a single piece of my own. The high ceilings in my large studio made it a perfect place for *Jasmine*.

The opening was my first since my relationship with Ellen had begun. Though my involvement with setting up the show had left me without any free time to give to Ellen, or to attend to her needs, I missed her not being there. Ellen and Sylvie were nothing alike, and my relationship with Ellen was totally different than my relationship with my ex-wife. Yet, though estranged and hostile as we were, Sylvie's boycott of my shows– after the one where we'd met– hurt me. Viewed rationally, Ellen's career was just as important to her as mine was to me, and I knew she cared about me and my feelings. There was a sense, however, that Ellen thought my painting was an obstacle between us, something else vying for my attention.

Sometimes I'm wrong.

Ellen came back from St. Martin tanned and in love. She spent her business trip thinking about me and us, and realized that she was in love with me, very much in love with me. Bringing me dozens of silly little presents, she wouldn't let me out of her sight for days. I liked Ellen very much– admired her mind, reveled in her body, and never had a dull moment with her– but I didn't feel anything that could be identified as love. We had started our relationship as two fortyish single people who enjoyed each other enough to spend our free time together. The rules and the expectations had changed without my knowing. I had been stupid, or at the least, naive, to think we could stay at our original level forever.

The fiasco with Sylvie had crippled me in the commitment department. Maybe even in the love department. Here was Ellen, declaring her absolute and eternal love for me, and any way I reacted was going to be interpreted as either cruel or unresponsive. Her avowal of love left me in a difficult predicament. She was a great woman who didn't deserve to be hurt, and her hard, bronzed body was difficult to reject or ignore.

When somebody swears their love for you, there is only one response that won't get you in trouble. You have to say– and say it as an immediate reflex with absolutely no hesitation– that you love them, too. I couldn't say that to Ellen if I didn't mean it, and I didn't mean it. My reluctance wasn't a moral decision, it was a survival instinct.. Once those words were said, there was no going back. Not with Ellen. I didn't say anything and Ellen absorbed my silence.

We tried to continue as before, but everything she said or did was permeated with dissatisfaction– which caused an ever increasing strain between us. Instead of just enjoying our time together, we had those soul-searching conversations that couples who are on different wavelengths often have. Neither of us had a better alternative, so we persevered.

I fugued just before Christmas and it lasted until New Year's Day. Though we had talked about my fugues many times, Ellen was unprepared for the experience– you have to live through one to understand. To complicate the situation, she had made lots and lots of holiday plans, most of which involved me.

When her many calls went unanswered, she became enraged, assuming I had skipped town on her. Maybe I was skipping out on her altogether, and was too much of a coward to confront her, or maybe I was just trying to avoid all the holiday parties to which she had committed us. Our relationship was in a deep trough, so fragile and vulnerable that we were both poised to, and willing to misinterpret and to suffer hurt feelings. She was pained and she was pissed. Scarred veteran of my fugues himself, Mo tried to reassure her and calm her down when she called him on the fourth day.. After she hung up, Mo scratched his head and upped the prices on my remaining unsold paintings. He had learned that they were now an extinct breed.

Ellen avoided my calls for a week. That was just as well because the aftermath of the fugue had launched me into a frenzy of a new series of paintings. When she deemed that there were enough messages on her answering machine to demonstrate my contrition, Ellen called me. We apologized to each other and resumed our now tenuous relationship. Things got worse and worse.

Toward the end of February, Mo asked me to stop by at the studio of a young artist who had caught his interest. I hated doing that kind of thing for every reason you can think, but finally agreed to look at the work.

David Stearns studio was nearby to my own. He was a harried, ticky, nervous man who exuded an air of insecurity in both his work and himself. Although most artists are insecure and self-conscious about their work, David Stearns took these shortcomings to a higher plane. He had talent, and his subject matter was different and stimulating. Whatever his personal flaws, he had that one imperative quality for an artist. His work made you want to look again.

Mo agreed. "But it may not be enough, Leo. David needs some kind of push to get him to the next level, and to give him some self-confidence. I'd like you to help."

"Me? I'm no mentor, nor do I know the first thing about teaching art. Besides, to be successful, your ideas must come from within. They can't be borrowed. Believe me, I know. It took me years to find ideas that worked for me."

"I'm not talking about anything like that. What I'm talking about is a two-man show. You still have four paintings left from before your last fugue that have never been shown. They'll sell on their own, but what if I did a two-man show with both his work and your four pieces? At least people would come."

"Is that fair to him?"

"I don't know what's fair, I just know that times have changed since *Schoolbuses*. I wouldn't be able to get people to your first show if I was putting it on today. It's a chance for him and no risk for you."

By the end of the morning, I'd agreed.

"Okay, but you have to promise to play me down in the advertising and let him have the spotlight."

Dara called two nights later. We hadn't spoken since the *Jasmine* opening, and with my early post-fugue obsessive painting, and the roller-coaster relationship with Ellen that used up all the rest of my time, I hadn't thought about Dara in months.

"Leo? Dara Harrington. Am I disturbing you?"

"Not at all. I don't answer if I'm working."

"I'm the team manager for the show you're doing with, er (she paused, probably to consult her notes) David Stearns. Mo said that you had definite ideas about how it should be advertised."

"Team manager? Is that a promotion?"

"I've been the manager since that famous cover you and Mo love so much. Anyway, what did you have in mind?"

I told her what I had told Mo– that I wanted David to be played up and my work played down– essentially his show with, maybe, a little reflected eclat from me.

"Is he any good?"

"You should go see for yourself. After all, you've got the eyes."

"What do you mean *the eyes*?"

"Don't you know?"

"What are you talking about?"

"Never mind."

"You know you're not allowed to do that. What eyes?"

"Your eyes. They're very special. When you look at something, you really look; and see. You mean no one's ever told you that? Your gaze is very compelling. If the advertizing gig doesn't pan out for you, you'd make a great hypnotist."

"Is this a compliment, or do you think I'm some sort of freak?"

"Very much a compliment. And, besides, you know art. Go see him and let me know what you think." Whoa, Leo, are you flirting?

Dara called a meeting at Mo's at the end of the week to make sure we were all in agreement about the advertising. The head copywriter on the project was there too. He was a personable and quick-witted man named Evan something. The two of them were professionals who knew what they were doing, and I was happy to excuse myself from the planning to get back to what I do best. Painting.

And overcame the need to paint Dara's haunting eyes.

Chapter 4

A couple of weeks after my lunch with Evan and Dara, Ellen and I were invited to a cocktail party at Pat's apartment to celebrate her sister's engagement. I had forgotten about the connection between Pat and Dara until I saw Dara at the party. Ellen and Pat were the only other people I knew at the party, so Dara's presence was a welcome relief from the boredom. Talking to Dara would be a number of steps up from my recent conversations with Ellen. We no longer spoke about anything except us.

While wandering around Pat's apartment pretending to look at the art work on the walls– which were mass produced and awful– Dara came up behind me. For some reason, her approach made me feel awkward. Dara helped me out.

"There's an artist's reflex. Put a glass of wine in your hand and you start looking at the walls."

"You caught me. You know, this is how I met my wife."

"At an engagement party?"

"No, at an opening, while I was looking at the walls."

"So you *can* be distracted."

"Looking away from the paintings that night was a huge mistake. I'm surprised I can still attend openings."

"That bad?"

"Ancient history. I don't even know why I thought of it."

"Are you and Ellen . . . ?"

"We're still together. She's over there somewhere. Oh, you mean, are we . . . ?"

We laughed because neither of us could say the words. Or, at least, that's why I laughed. I was almost sure that's why Dara laughed too. It was nice to be silly. Ellen and I hadn't had a light conversation since she had come back from the Caribbean. It was nice being silly with Dara.

"My real reason for looking at the walls is because I had nothing better to do. I'm not having a very good time here. Will you come have some coffee with me? Or are you with someone?" I looked around the room for someone with a sign, I suppose, saying "I'm with Dara."

"I'm alone, but what about Ellen?"

"Please?" We slipped out, unnoticed.

The coffee never happened. We walked around for hours, talking and laughing. At three in the morning, we ended up in front of Dara's apartment.

"How about that coffee, now? " she asked.

"It's kind of late and . . ."

"Ellen?"

"No, my painting. I like to get an early start. As for Ellen, I think I made a really good friend tonight. I should be allowed to do that. You and I have nothing to do with me and Ellen."

"Will she agree?"

"I'm not sure that it matters."

"We may both live to regret this."

"Maybe. But not so far. Right now, it seems like an acceptable risk."

Dara and I had lunch together that next week, then I began meeting her after work to walk her home. From something that occurred every few days without planning or routine, it escalated to a daily activity as my walks with Dara became my favorite part of the day. My painting totally engrosses me, so that wasn't a problem. But whenever I took a break to clean brushes or give my hand a rest, I thought about Dara. Thought about her a lot.

For all their unchartered electricity, our walks were innocent. We walked and talked for the mile or so to Dara's house, said goodnight, and parted.

A week or two after we started these daily walks, Dara extended a nonspecific invitation to meet her daughter sometime. I wasn't anxious to leave her company, so accompanied her up to her apartment right then. The charged energy that passed between Dara and me was unlike anything I had ever experienced, and though I knew I was breaching a trust with Ellen, it no longer mattered. I would deal with Ellen when I had to.

This is when and where it happened. The moment that a twelve-year-old girl made me ride the elevator up to her apartment accompanied by her mother who was falling in love with me. Leo and Dara, and in a little while, Gwen. Everything before this moment is background, so that you know who I am. Everything beyond this point is what it's all about.

Chapter 5

At twelve, Gwen was a cute little blonde who looked nothing like her darker mother. In the beginning, I never really got past Dara's eyes to look at the rest of her. They demanded special attention. Now, looking at her from my perspective as both an artist and a potential lover– !!!– I realized that she was a beautiful woman. She had shoulder-length chestnut hair, and angular features that resisted the temptation toward severity, rather giving her an air of competence.

Dara was the kind of woman who would do that– want a man whom she liked to meet Gwen, and say nothing about that man to her daughter until she brought him home. Not that it was a common occurrence. Years had passed since Dara had let herself like someone. Maybe that was the reason Dara needed to introduce me to Gwen, and why Gwen needed to meet me.

We were both shy during our first meeting. Dara kept things light and moving, and Gwen survived the initial awkwardness without any major trauma.

"Why don't you go do your homework? I'll call you for dinner," Dara said when all the initial *how-ya-doin's?* were done. To me she said, "Can I get you a drink?"

"Yes, if you're having one."

We took our wineglasses to the living room, continuing our conversation from the walk home, which was about my concerns about my first two-man show.

"I heard you were changing genres again."

The word didn't sound so pretentious when Dara used it.

"That's never a conscious decision. When it happens, I don't have a choice."

Dara knew all about my fugues and the post-fugue changes that occur.

"How do you know this stuff?"

"I told you, I'm a fan. I know your paintings, and I know about your life."

"That's a little spooky, but I'm very flattered." I was.

"You're very special."

I wanted to ask, but knew enough not to. For now, basking was enough. Before leaving, we kissed for the first time– a brief and light kiss, but a kiss nonetheless. I floated home like a teenager in love.

Matters with Ellen were getting worse on their own, and my growing friendship with Dara– okay, more than friendship– was accelerating the decline. In the middle of those interminable discussions with Ellen, my mind wandered off to thoughts of Dara. The microscopic examination of what I wanted out of life was something best left to college dorm rooms in the middle of the night, not something to obsess over in middle age. I wanted to paint free from the bother of everyday annoyances, and have fun when I wasn't painting. Anything else was just an accumulation of irrelevance.

As her misery took control of her, Ellen showed up, unannounced, at all times of the day, and even in the middle of the night with one emotional crisis or insightful epiphany after another. How many different ways could we talk about the same dead-end relationship we had? I had no more thoughts on the subject. I was talked out. I was becoming Ellen-ed out.

There was nothing left. No small remnant to sustain the pretense that we shared a mutually satisfying relationship. We stopped having sex, as Ellen put it, *until this was all settled*, and never went out anymore. We had stayed together for the last few months out of inertia and lack of alternatives. Now, there was Dara who, at least for now, was undemanding of my time and my soul. Though Ellen and I continued to see each other on our usual schedule, we no longer did anything when we were together. I painted and she sat around the studio depressed.

The walks with Dara were becoming full evenings.. Occasionally, I got involved in a painting and didn't show up at the end of the day. Dara never called to check on me; we resumed where we had left off on the next day, or whenever we saw each other again.

Unused to such freedom, I asked Dara about it, and she replied, "I just presume that you're seeing another canvas," and laughed. Her self-assuredness and her easy manner prompted me to ask her opinion about what I should do with regard to Ellen.

"Like I'm really going to jump in here and fuck myself. I'm not exactly a disinterested party to you and Ellen. Ask Mo, ask Barbara. Leave me out of this one."

No matter in what hypothetical context I framed the question, Dara wouldn't comment on Ellen and me.

Things with Dara kept improving as things with Ellen got worse and worse. Convinced, at first, that the two situations weren't related, my self delusion couldn't stand the evidence for long. Breaking up with Ellen was inevitable, but except for Sylvie, my previous romances had all dwindled into a natural death that didn't require a formal parting. Inexperienced with disentanglement, a quick and honest break appeared to be my best option.

Ellen didn't take the news well. We were stuck in the same rut, so she should have welcomed the end as much as I did.

"I can't give you what you want, or what you need."

"That's what you're supposed to say. It's what every man is taught to say while he's ripping out a woman's heart."

Ellen's presence– forgotten clothes, hairpins, books she had left behind– lingered in my apartment for weeks. Her emotional presence faded within days.

Chapter 6

My relationship with Dara was easy and uncluttered by anything except the two of us. We shared an uncanny intimacy– thinking alike and feeling alike about everything– though we still hadn't had sex. Sex was the obvious next step for me, but Dara held back. Intellectually, we were welded, but she continued her reluctance to initiate the physical side of our relationship. Besides, there was no way to accomplish sex at Dara's with Gwen always there.

"You've never asked to see my studio."

"You're right. It's such a cliche; and I don't want that to be who we are. I've come on to you like some love-stricken groupie, and I'm trying to hold on to a little self-esteem. You're asking me to have sex with you. It's flashing neon. For sure, we're overdue, it's just that I didn't want to merely "have sex" with you. You're too special to me."

"That's an uncomfortable paradox. Would sex be that bad?"

"Only in that way. There are things you should know about me."

"What do you mean?"

"I made a big mistake in college by getting into drugs right away. Not just experimenting or dabbling, I was always on something.

With the drugs came sex. Those two things consumed me so much that there was no time for anything else.

"During sophomore year, I dropped out of school and stopped talking to my parents. I became obsessed with having sex with everyone I could, and I stayed so drugged up that the pleasure was no longer the impetus.

"When I discovered that I was pregnant, and decided to keep Gwen, I realized that it was time to make changes in my life. That meant a steady job and a home in which to raise her.

"I'm a totally different person than I was back then. Still, sex is a reminder of an empty and self-destructive time in my life. Of course I want to have sex with you, Leo, I just don't want to rush into it. Let's let it happen slowly in the evolution of our relationship, rather than let it become its foundation." I heard the *of course I want to have sex with you* part.

"Will you come to my studio, if I promise we'll keep our clothes on?"

"Gwen's sleeping at a friend's house tomorrow night. I'll come over when you're finished painting. After the tour, we can have our first real date."

As promised, there was no sex that night, although when Dara first saw Jasmine hanging in the studio, she held me close to her for a long time and something almost happened.

We were together as much as we could manage, growing closer and closer and sharing everything except our bodies. The closer I got to Dara, the more impatient I became. The time had long passed when it should have happened, and it was unnatural and forced that it hadn't. My experience with Ellen made me reluctant to talk about it for fear of analyzing our relationship to death.

Dara was the one who brought it up.

"I guess I'm more dysfunctional than I thought."

"In general, or is there something specific?"

"I love you, Leo." We had never actually spoken those words, but it was true.

"I love you, too." The sentiment flowed this time.

"So why am I having so much trouble with the sex thing? Or maybe it's because I love you so much. It's all so complicated and stupid. Sex became so robotic and ungratifying to me that I feel it would demean our relationship to make love. And yet, I've never felt so close to anyone. Making love with you should feel so natural and right."

"This is way out of my league. I have no idea what to tell you, and I'm not saying I'm going to like it, it's just that I'm so into you that whatever you need, I'll do. How long has it been?"

"Eight or nine years. Not a conscious decision, more from circumstance than by choice. I've dated off and on since Gwen was born, but nothing serious or even remotely interesting. There's slim pickings for an aging, single mother in Manhattan. So I don't know what I would have done if the opportunity had come up."

"I'm not going to push you. You let me know when you're ready. As for me, my torment will be suffered in silence. In the meantime, remember that I really do love you and want us to be together."

We kissed. Kissing and hugging was never a problem. We did lots and lots of kissing and hugging. Dara was very into kissing and hugging. She stopped there.

As time went on, and a lot of it did, my sexual frustration was manifest in my paintings. There had been long periods of time in which I went without sex during my adult life, but never while with someone I loved. My canvases became seething tableaus of

35

unrequited lust and sensuality. The message wasn't lost on Dara. She made herself scarce for a while.

The paintings were selling as fast as I could produce them. There was an energy in them that was like the hot lava in my work during the Sylvie wars. This time, however, I was more in control and better able to channel the craziness. My work consumed me until all else stopped being important.

I painted.

Talking about it wasn't going to help. We had done that, and nothing had changed. Time went on and nothing changed.

I painted.

One night, after Dara and I had been together for three months, she came over earlier than expected, and we sat on the sofa in my studio talking while waiting for our dinner reservation. Dara leaned forward to get her wineglass. As she did, her shirt rode up, revealing a stretch of her lower back. Without thinking, I placed my hand on the smooth, soft skin above the waistband like I had done many times before. Her skin quickened beneath my fingers, and the touch became a caress.

Dara leaned back and closed her eyes, enjoying the moment. My hand continued to stroke as Dara's breathing got deeper and guttural, like the sounds she made as she was falling asleep.

It was as though neither of us knew we were making love until it was over. The act was so fluid and self-contained.

Sex with Sylvie had been passionate and acrobatic, like an aerobics class. The two of us were exhausted and sweating when we were done,. Finishing was almost a relief.

Sex with Ellen was a well-choreographed pas de deux– with a beginning and a passion building second movement that climaxed, as it is meant to climax, and then ended in a gentle denouement. We were left with a sense of accomplishment.

Sex with Dara was on a different plane. An alpha state, a Zen experience, and well worth the wait. We became each other and we became an *us* being.

For a while, all we could do was to hum at each other.

"Hmm."

"Hmm." Snuggling into each other, savoring the oneness, both unwilling to break the connection.

One would think that this simple act would have turned the tide, would have redefined the way we were together. We had been deeply in love before we had sex, and sex had been sublime, had done nothing to alter that love. One would have been wrong.

Making love with Dara made me want to make love again. But Dara was satiated for months. Making love always just happened, without planning for it, and never speaking its name out loud. Months went by until the stars and the moon and all the gods in heaven had aligned themselves in some mystical pattern before Dara allowed herself to slip into sex. Despite the long intervals, or because of them, it was always great.

Sex was Dara's fatal flaw, and I was determined not to let it slay our relationship. Dara's avoidance of sex was the defect that marred her perfection, and therefore made her more real and obtainable. How I wished it had been something simpler. Like snoring.

She was as confused as I was, but rejected the idea of counseling because it was so counter to her take-charge personality. Dwelling on our almost nonexistent sex life was only going to make sex too important and the emphasis would be counterproductive– Dara wasn't able to distinguish between de-emphasizing sex and no sex at all. She suggested, with convincing sincerity, that I have sex with other women. I didn't want other women, I wanted Dara. That wasn't going to happen. Either way.

Chapter 7

She was a normal teenager from a normal suburban home outside of Philadelphia. Her father, though not a musician himself, was the secretary for the Philadelphia Philharmonic Orchestra. Her mother was a housewife who divided her time between bridge and garden clubs. Dara's main concerns were clothes, boys and her high school yearbook, for which she was the Art Editor. Dara and her older sister had a cordial, but mutually disinterested relationship.

Graduating fifth in her high school class, Dara was going to Cornell University where she would major in art while waiting for the right man to come along. They would marry after graduation, and her role would be to provide him with love and support while he pursued a brilliant career. The young wife would devote herself to their beautiful house and beautiful children who would, when they grew up, continue the family traditions of affluent suburbia.

Her transition from all-American girl-next-door to militant hippie began almost as soon as her trunk came to a complete rest on the floor of her dorm room at Cornell. Her freshman roommate, a physics major from New York, was stoned for the entire fall semester, and never made it past the first set of finals– gone before the first snow fell in Ithaca. Her main accomplishment at college was turning Dara on to smoking pot.

The graduate student who taught Dara's freshman English tutorial hit on Dara within the first week of classes, and Dara hit right back. He was handsome and older, brilliant and sophisticated in comparison to the somewhat sheltered Dara who actually believed that she could have the same kind of mostly innocent relationship with him that she'd had with her high school boyfriends. He called himself Chip because in the mid-sixties people still had those nicknames. Chip introduced Dara to sex and hallucinogens. Dara was indefatigable in her pursuit and experimentation with both. Her new boyfriend's main interests were John Donne, acid and mescaline, and he only wanted to have sex when they were both tripping. The freshman girl, open to all new experiences, was happy to comply.

The Chip happening wore thin very soon. He was doing more and more drugs, which changed him from a fascinating mentor into a nonperson. Dara loved her art courses and wanted to do well enough to progress to studio work. She controlled her drug intake in order to maintain some of her ability to concentrate.

Those were the times, however, when the student body was divided into those firmly rooted in the fifties tradition– fraternity parties, beer drinking, football games, mixers– and the dope smoking, acid tripping, protest marching students of the early seventies. Anyone who used pot was automatically a brother/sister of anyone else who smoked pot even if they had, otherwise, nothing in common.

Suddenly, Dara found herself amidst a contingent of friends who were drugged, sexually indiscriminate, and very political. Pot was ubiquitous. Hallucinogens and group sex were the norms for weekends. As an artist, she was expected to trip regularly, and

Dara had no problems with any of the trappings of her new lifestyle. College was a blast.

One of her more regular sex partners was also one of the founders of the Cornell SDS chapter, which Dara joined even though she had no personal politics.

Her return home, that first Thanksgiving in college, marked the beginning of the fragmentation of her relationship with her family, especially her mother. In less than a semester, the archetypical girl-next-door had become the stereotypical hippie– too new at it to do more than spout the basic tenets of the party line.

Dara's father was both amused and annoyed. Amused at Dara's change from a naive high school girl to an exploring college student. Annoyed with her sweeping self-righteous rejection of her family's values and lifestyle.

Her mother was not amused. Not at all. Their daughter was disgusting and abrasive with long and wild hair. Dara's wardrobe consisted of poorly fitted jeans and assorted peasant blouses. Her armpits were unshaven. And she went braless!

The hippie girl put down her mother for everything – for living in a beautiful house *while children were starving.* For being involved in her clubs *while young American boys were being killed in a jungle someplace in Asia.* For wanting her daughters to be pretty and ladylike *so I can land a rich husband and be just like you?*

The conflict between Dara and her mother lost all of its political content, degenerating into a purely personal denunciation of the other's values. Dara, like her sister before her, had been the perfect daughter– bright, pretty, artistic and popular. Mother and daughter loved to shop together and talk about an idyllic future for Dara. Now, they had become politically incorrect icons to one another decades before the phrase was even coined. The rift had begun.

Dara returned to school exasperated but smug. That Thanksgiving was the last holiday that she ever spent with her family. The year was 1967, and the antiwar movement was gaining momentum. Dara enjoyed the protest marches and demonstrations, mostly for the sex and drugs that erupted afterwards. She was arrested several times, which was just another part of the whole experience. When things escalated to the destruction of government offices using guns and explosives, the protests stopped being a lark. The young art student became disenchanted with the politics of it all.

The counterculture had evolved by then, so Dara had more than one option. This forced her to think about her social and political perspective and develop a personal world view. Dara's priorities were her drawing (she was already leaning toward graphic design), drugs (the higher, the better) and sex (the more and the weirder, the better).

She limited her friendships to other artists who were morally committed to the evolving ideas regarding war, race, and sex, but who were politically inactive. They took the position that they had a gift to share with the new world order when it came. Right now, they were too busy developing their gift to get involved with the drudgery of establishing that order. The uninspired, unliberated old guard art professors who were supposed to be their teachers were a hindrance to their gift, and they could learn more from each other, and from life itself, and from the free expression of their Art..

Adopting the attitude of her peers, Dara dropped out of school in the middle of her sophomore year and went to live at a poorly organized commune on a farm outside Ithaca. There was a core of fifteen regulars with as many as thirty to forty others living with them at any given time. Most everyone's time was spent doing drugs while dabbling in their respective art; very little commune work ever got done. Despite the original goal of self-sufficiency, they needed money for food and rent and drugs.

Once or twice a week, Dara put on a dress—and a bra— and shoes, and went to work at a struggling area ad agency where she filled in doing whatever they needed that day. Despite poor pay, she learned a lot about the mechanics of the business and practiced her graphic skills under formal guidelines with deadlines and strict format requirements. The hours at the agency honed her talent much more than the society of the dysfunctional artists whose inspiration she was supposed to share.

The rest of her time, however, her life was consumed with drugs. While the other artists experimented with oils and watercolors, Dara used sex as the medium with which to vent her creative urges. She was the local sex machine; willing to have sex with anyone, anywhere, at any time, and with whatever bizarre embellishments they could invoke. As the drugs took over, the sex became less gratifying, but her nothing's-too-outrageous image became even more important to her, and her sexual activity, now devoid of everything, escalated. Out of control, she was obsessed with cramming as many drugs and sexual partners into her day as she could manage.

In the midst of the driven emptiness of her life, she became pregnant. Dara went out into a field with a couple of tabs of acid to get in touch with her fetus. Whatever transpired during that conversation, Dara decided to keep the baby and never took another drug again.

Dara's parents refused to help. She hadn't spoken to them in several years, and the sudden news of her unmarried pregnancy by an unknown father solidified their disapproval. To compound her predicament, her sister had lived the proper life with an accountant husband and two legitimate children. She was on her own.

Homeless, penniless and pregnant, Dara had no place to go. There were no shelters for women at that time. Unwilling to remain at the commune with all its temptations, she found a cousin in New Jersey who let Dara stay with her during the pregnancy. Dara commuted to Manhattan every day to do temp jobs at various ad and public relations agencies.. She worked hard and sucked knowledge and technique from the experienced graphic artists with whom she worked. As with drugs and alcohol, once Dara committed herself, she committed all the way. Her work ethic and talent were noticed by her supervisors– one offered her a full-time job after Gwen was born.

Dara needed to work. Because day care was still more of a concept than a reality at that time, there was no one with whom to leave Gwen, near their home. With no other options, Dara toted the infant Gwen back and forth from her apartment in New Jersey to Manhattan where a few day care programs operated.

Gwen was such a joy to her that Dara didn't let the drudgery of caring for an infant, working full time, and commuting with an infant in her arms get her down. Advancement in her career was the best way out for her, so she applied herself to that task and soon became an invaluable member of her team.

The young mother never spoke to her own mother after the day she told her parents about her pregnancy. She called home after Gwen was born to tell her parents about their new granddaughter. Her father was cold to her, and she never spoke to him again either. It was unlike her father to behave that way on his own. He must have succumbed to her mother, who had declared Dara persona non grata in the family. Her father would have abided by that decision.

After several pay raises, Dara was able to hire a full-time babysitter for Gwen at home. Eventually, she moved to Manhattan where Dara divided her time between work and Gwen. Rarely dating, she limiting her circle of friends to work colleagues with whom she did nothing outside of the office.

Dara's main recreational event was going to art galleries and museums where she pushed Gwen around in her stroller while viewing the artwork. She took a particular liking to a young rising New York artist for whom, one day, she would design a brochure.

Chapter 8

Gwen was wary and hostile at first, which made me feel uncomfortable when I was at Dara's. The feeling wasn't by accident. The twelve-year-old intended for me to react that way, distancing herself from her own needs. I tried not to force myself on her, and we gave each other a lot of room. As time went on, we lapsed into a fragile truce and then, little by little, got to know one another.

Whatever resentment I might have developed towards her aggressive sullenness, she *was* Dara's daughter, so I liked her for that reason alone.

Time and patience softened her attitude. My celebrity status gave me an aura that was appealing to a preteen. Her friends' parents all knew who I was and, the few times that we were together in public, I was often recognized and approached. Not quite rock star status and nowhere as cool, but it was something.

Gwen had grown up with no male presence in her life and little girls need a father. Since I was the only man who had lasted around Dara, she gravitated towards a relationship with me, especially since I diluted Dara's autocratic mothering, which could be oppressive at times. Dara encouraged her daughter's growing reliance on my intervention in a dispute.

And then there was the way Dara felt about me. Even a preteen had to notice the change in her mother when I was around. Dara was happier, and therefore more carefree around the house.

As we got more comfortable with each other, Gwen often asked me to help her with her homework or a school project, and sought my male perspective on matters, mostly fantasized, of the heart. We spent afternoons together when she had a half-day at school and Dara was working. If I was going to be a part of Dara's life, I would have to be a part of Gwen's life as well, so it had to be everyone's decision.

Dara and Gwen were opposites. Dara was dark, Gwen was blonde. Dara was self-confident and poised, while Gwen was insecure and awkward. Dara was thin and lithe, Gwen chubby and clumsy. Gwen suffered from being Dara's daughter. She was sweet and pretty, but she lacked spark or drive. Few things got her excited. Few things held her interest.

Spending the day with Gwen had a typical form– a movie followed by either a video or music store where she allowed me to overindulge her. One afternoon when we met, she surprised me.

"Can we go to a museum today?" I was excited that Gwen was showing interest in something.

"Which one?"

"I don't know. One that I'll like. All I know is that you're famous, nothing about what you do."

We went to the Museum of Modern Art where Gwen seemed more puzzled than anything else. None of the artwork got to her or made her stop to look again. She barely acknowledged my painting when I pointed it out to her. Still, it was a start and it was nice that we were getting to feel easy with each other and enjoying each other's company. Dara wasn't there when we got back home. Sometimes she worked late.

We had dinner together at a café in Soho where the arty crowd mingled. Gwen felt very sophisticated. Afterwards, we walked most of the way home and talked like we never had before. At last, we were becoming friends on our own. Although Dara wasn't home when I dropped Gwen off, she assured me that she would be fine by herself, and sent me on my way.

Dara laid it on me as soon as I saw her the next day.

"I had sex last night."

"I'm sorry I wasn't there," forcing the joke despite the distinct knot building in my stomach.

"With Marty. One of those zipless things. All passion and body fluids that meant nothing to either one of us."

"So I guess that leaves only me." Her words made me nauseated and achy, like I'd been kicked in the balls. The implications of Dara's causal affair with her boss cascaded around me, overwhelming me. It was too soon to think about what she had just told me. I just stood there feeling stupid and miserable.

"What are you going to do?" Dara wasn't prepared for my reaction. What had she expected?

"What I always do, paint." The temporary solution was simple because it was my solution for everything. "I love you, Dara, so in the long run, this isn't going to matter. Right now, though, I don't even know how to look at it. If we had a normal sexual relationship and you had sex with someone else, I don't think it would have mattered at all. But, us . . . this . . . I don't know what I want to say, I'm just ranting, so I better not say anything. I'm just going to paint for a while."

The hurt was an unnamed entity surfacing through the numbness. Better not to think about it at all. I was so shaken that I didn't want to think about anything, not even about painting. That's how bad it was. I called Mo to insist that he have a drink with me.

Mo had his own problems that were worse than mine. After more than thirty-five years of marriage, almost forty of living and working together, Barbara wanted a divorce. They had worked hard for years, and now that they were getting older, it was time to slow down a little. Their daughter, Lee, was with them at the gallery now. Lee had an MBA from Wharton and had majored in art history as an undergraduate at Bennington. She was smart and personable, and not only was Mo presently grooming her to take over the gallery, she had grown up in the business and had a built-in understanding of how everything worked.

Mo wasn't ready to retire and Barbara was. Both children were into their careers. Maurice (Momo) was an orthopedic surgeon in his second year of residency in Salt Lake City. Barbara thought it was time to step away from the business and enjoy themselves. She had wanted to do it with Mo, but when he kept putting her off, she decided to do it anyway.

Mo wasn't ready to let either Barbara or the gallery go. The distraction of this unsolvable dilemma prevented him from providing the sympathetic shoulder I needed. His problems depressed me even more than my own, so I drank enough to take the edge off both.

I painted.

I had two havens. Painting was my haven from the world. The world didn't exist when there was an unfinished canvas before me. But, sometimes, it was the painting I needed to escape. Dara had been a haven from myself and my painting. Dara wasn't an option this time. So . . .

I painted.

With the status few artists ever attain in their lifetime, it hadn't been necessary to have a show for several years. Mo had a list of buyers waiting for my next canvas. As soon as they were completed, he made a few calls and the painting sold to the highest bidder.

I painted.

For six weeks, nonstop except for short periods of sleep. Dara left a message on my machine.

"I love you."

I left one back.

"I love you too, wait for me."

Gwen also left a message.

"Leo, it's Gwen . . . er . . . Gwen Harrington. Are you mad at us?"

Six weeks of continuous painting is a lot, even for me, and I had to pause. The world rushed in. Loneliness and emptiness engulfed me. I missed Dara. Nothing else mattered. The frenzied painting had accomplished its job– the issue of Dara's urgent and mindless sex with her boss at the same time that she was unmotivated and reluctant to have sex with me, was over without ever once consciously thinking about it. Maybe I had just barricaded it in one of the cul-de-sacs of my subconscious from which it would, one day, burst out and ruin everything.

Dara greeted me, where I waited for her outside her office, with hugs and kisses and some tears. I felt better just seeing her. Dara always made me feel better.

We walked arm and arm, but in silence, to Dara's apartment. Gwen greeted me with neither enthusiasm nor surprise, as if I had just returned from an errand after having been with her all day.

Dara maintained body contact, even while she opened and poured us some wine.

"Do you want to talk?" she asked.

"Not really. It's dead.   Some things aren't designed to be examined too closely."

"Well, I do. I've been rehearsing for weeks. Even though you think you can talk a relationship to death, I don't want this hanging over us. We need to come to terms . . ."

"We've got stuff hanging over us.   One more thing won't matter."

"You're getting angry. This is not at all what I rehearsed. I've been selfish and stupid about the sex thing. From now on we'll have sex whenever you want to."

"You don't get it, do you? I don't just want to have sex with you. I want you to want to have sex with me. You love me, I know that. But evidently I've never inspired mindless passion in you, passion you were more than capable of achieving with Marty. You can't decide to change that. You can't legislate passion. Passion happens, or it doesn't. Like with you and Marty."

"Marty was an aberration, you know that. There *is* no sex like sex with you. You know that, too. I never should have told you. I never should have done it. I want the whole thing to go away. I want to start over with you and not be such an asshole this time."

"Dara, you're the one I want. Dara Harrington. This Dara Harrington. Not some figment of either of our imaginations. When all is said and done, I'll take you any way you come. I don't want you to pretend anything for my sake. I want you to be Dara. I love Dara. With your past, with your hangups, with whatever. But even if that wasn't the case, we can't start over. We are who we are– who we were."

51

"Well, you've got me. You've always had me. From day one. Do you want to hear the rest?"

"No."

"I bought *Junction.*"

"You can't afford that!"

"Mo helped me."

"You still can't afford it. Give it back. You can have *Jasmine.*"

"I want something I can look at every day, when you're not here. I need the contact. I realized that when I didn't see you for so long."

"I'll talk to Mo."

Chapter 9

Mo, who was always trying to protect me from myself, had me set up a trust that bought *Junction*. The painting would go to Dara at my death, but remain mine in the meantime. Dara resisted at first, but agreed to the arrangement if I let her pay the legal fees.

After my self-imposed exile, we reverted to our previous relationship. The only difference was that every few months, Dara called me to remind me that she would be coming over. The phone call was a signal that she wanted me to initiate sex.. We never spoke about sex, we just "let it happen," but now we were doing it on cue. The new 'arrangement' was as close as we got to a normal relationship, and it wasn't very close at all.

Over the next six months, I had a series of fugues, lasting only two or three days each time, but occurring almost every two weeks. By the time I started a painting, I fugued and lost interest in it, therefore got no work done. My doctors ordered another series of tests, to no avail. One doctor thought I might have a bipolar disorder– painting was the manic phase, the fugues an unusual form of the depressive phase. Lithium interfered with my painting, and because the fugues were so random, I couldn't tell if it had any effect on them, so I stopped.

During the same time, Dara's company announced that it was relocating to Long Island. They would maintain executive offices in Manhattan with a skeleton crew, but the important production work would all be done in Northport. Dara was offered a private office, a large raise and moving costs. She accepted.

Gwen was barely getting by, academically, at her private school in Manhattan, and she had made only one friend in eight years. She wasn't even particularly attached to that one girl. Dara hoped that Gwen would do better in a new setting and at a different school.

At sixteen, she had shed her pubescent chubbiness, becoming tall and thin. Gwen would have been very pretty except that her vacuous, mostly dour face wasn't attractive. Dr. Anne Jamison, Gwen's psychologist, felt that Gwen had suffered from living in the shadow of Dara's confidence and my fame. On the other hand, she seemed to like us both and sought our company more than she shunned it. The doctor couldn't answer our most important question. Was her lack of energy and her failure to generate interest in anything a normal, passing teenage phase, or a sign of a deeper problem?

Gwen's troubled beauty, along with her precociously large breasts, were provocative enough to get her asked out by the high school boys, but few called more than once, and no one more than twice.

Dara hoped that the move to Northport would have a positive effect on the teenager. Besides the panacea of fresh air, their new life would be more comfortable. Dara's salary would increase, as well as her position and her say in company policy. The only one who might possibly suffer from this move was me. The train ride from Manhattan to Northport took two hours, so there was no way I could continue to paint and still see Dara as frequently as I used to, and needed to.

"Why don't you move too? There's nothing to keep you here. And this neighborhood is getting worse and worse every day." She never liked it.

"You mean, with you?"

"Not to live together. You don't need me or Gwen getting in your way when you're painting, and even after all of these years, your fugues still freak me. I need a place to be when you're in one, and I can't even imagine what it would be like for Gwen. But there's no reason why we can't live close to each other. I don't want to see you any less than I do now."

The place I found– and found before Dara bought a house– was an abandoned warehouse near the old port–easily converted into a good-sized living area and a large studio, which I remodeled with lots of skylights and large windows on three walls so I could almost always paint by natural light. Because of the light and the dampness, and keeping the studio comfortably warm, the plants I filled it with stayed lush and green. Dara called my studio "the rain forest."

Dara later found a nice Victorian house and made a second career of decorating it, but the finished product was beautiful as well as comfortable. *Junction* was shown amid surroundings that enhanced it. Dara was very happy.

We didn't see much of each other for two months because my new studio wasn't finished, so I stayed in Manhattan to paint while Dara moved to Northport to work. She was so busy with the new house and the demands of her new office that we couldn't get together often.

Sylvie phoned me just before I moved, after fifteen years of exile to the suburbs. She was all but gone from my active memory, but her voice called forth misshapen thoughts from a dead past.

"Leo? It's Sylvie. How are you, Leo?"

"Fine, Sylvie. What do you want?"

"Can't I just call to say hello?"

"After all these years? I don't think so. I'm kind of busy right now. If you're just calling to chat, I don't have the time or the inclination."

"I'd like to be your friend."

"What's the matter, your marriage going sour? The time to be my friend was when *we* were married."

"I'm sorry that I wasn't. You might have been the right one for me, after all. We all make choices. Mine was giving up my career for love and a family. I've discovered that I wasn't cut out to be a mother, and very bad at faking it. Love is, as it turns out, no substitute for a successful career."

"This sounds like where I come in."

"I'd just like to see you, is all."

"That's not going to happen, Sylvie. I don't want to. Besides, I'm moving to the Island soon."

"Then, would you talk to Mo? See if he can help me get back into the business?"

"You know Mo well enough to talk to him yourself."

"But he hates me."

"No more than I do. Good-bye."

Sylvie was the last person I wanted to reenter my life. Now, or ever. Hatred was the right word. Not the wrenching hatred from the end of our marriage. That passed after a while. Time hadn't done anything to soften the passive hate. I learned to hate Sylvie when I was married to her and didn't know Dara, didn't have Dara for comparison. Talking about those two women in the same sentence was almost sacrilege, and disheartening to think that Sylvie had once been my wife.

Finally, though, my studio was completed. Dara lived just a few miles away from me, and after all these years, I learned to drive. Dara bought me everything I needed to set up my new home– things I never would have thought to buy until I discovered that I needed them. She even did all the decorating in the living quarters. I bought a drawing table and set up an area in my studio for her to use if she wanted to work alongside me.

We settled into a Bizzaro-world kind of matrimonial bliss: two separate homes, rare sex, but a great sense of oneness. We never fought and were both very busy with our work. Our main problem was our growing concern for Gwen.

Gwen was a senior in high school with no plans beyond that. She still had no interests. I had come to think of Gwen as our daughter, not just Dara's, and I had provided for her financial security. We wanted her to be happy and fulfilled, but that seemed unlikely unless she found something that could catch and hold her attention. Counseling had helped her identify the source of her problems– the feeling that she was unable to compete with Dara and me– but did nothing to resolve them.

Her graduation from high school was almost a nonevent. She didn't want to attend the ceremony and wouldn't have except that Dara and I said we would go with or without her. Dara had made it clear that Gwen had to do something– school or job, so Gwen got a summer job at the reception desk of a local motel.

She worked for as many hours as they would let her, then came straight home. Occasionally, she drove around the neighborhood for a few hours. Gwen spent her time alone or with us, but didn't seem particularly unhappy. That was Gwen's bane: she wasn't particularly anything.

In the fall, Dara suggested, in her typically forceful and don't-bother-to-pretend-you-won't-do-it-because-this-is-me way that only Dara could pull off, that Gwen enroll in a nearby community college. She continued to work at the motel as a caretaker/housekeeper during the winter months, but she agreed to take some classes at night.

Of course, she had no idea what subjects she wanted to study. In the next few years, she dropped– or took incompletes– in more courses than she finished, and still had no idea which field she wanted to pursue. The concept of *majoring* in something never registered in her brain. She kept her job at the motel out of inertia and fear of Dara's scorn, but was well-liked by the management towards whom she displayed her usual noncommital apathy.

Other than her total lack of direction, Gwen was the perfect daughter. She was a very nice young woman– kind and caring, didn't do drugs or drink even moderately. She occasionally had dates, but never sustained a relationship for more than a few weeks. Even she noticed.

"I think I may be a lesbian," she told us one night.

"Why do you think that?" (Dara)

"Men don't seem to stay interested in me, and I haven't met anyone I couldn't take or leave."

"But you feel that way about everything. Have you had sex with anyone, yet?" This was a rare conversation. Introspection was not Gwen's forte, so I seized upon the moment to keep her talking.

"Yeah, it was okay . . . but nothing special. I think I should at least try being with a woman."

"Is that what you want?" Dara said, looking at me sideways with her eyebrows arched. She was trying to remain cool and open-minded, but this conversation was not going well for her.

"Are you attracted to someone specific?" I asked the question Dara wanted to ask.

"No, not yet. There's no one I know whom I'd even consider, nor has another women ever approached me. I just thought maybe I should try it."

"Well, I'm probably going to end up in trouble for saying this, but I don't see any reason why you shouldn't satisfy your curiosity."

Dara and I discussed it alone, later that night.

"Maybe if I wasn't such a fucked-up, sexually dyslexic loser myself, my daughter would have a developed sexual identity and not be so fucked-up too. Why do we make such crippling choices for ourselves?"

"This is the same old thing, her inability to get involved. It's better that she at least explore some options rather than just be a blob."

"I'm not ready for this."

"No one ever is. Don't get too worked up until you know there's really something to be worked up about. I, for one, would welcome enthusiasm for just about anything."

Gwen never did have a lesbian experience and went on the way she always had. All of a sudden she was twenty-four.

Chapter 10

At twenty-four, Gwen lived alongside her own world rather than as part of it. Nothing impelled her or compelled her, and there was no place she wanted to go. Her life was dull and spiritless, and worst of all, it didn't seem to bother her. She had no friends and no interests– didn't read, didn't garden, didn't exercise. She simply was.

Neither Dara nor I could understand how she could be this way. We both had work that we loved– work that engrossed, motivated, and excited us. We also had each other. Such apathy; such an empty, aimless, dispassionate existence was beyond our imagination. Gwen wasn't stupid and she wasn't evil– evil would have been a step up, it would have been *something*. We flogged ourselves for doing that to her, spewing mumbo jumbo that we had learned from Dr. Jamison and Gwen's teachers. The scourging cemented our guilt, but did nothing to help Gwen.

There had to be something, some scenario, some person, some happenstance to ignite Gwen, but the specific event was difficult to imagine. She didn't pursue any interests that might pull her out of the quagmire and get her going because she didn't have any interests.

The likelihood of a deep and passionate love was remote because a deep love was related to having shared interests and goals.

Gwen had settled into a pattern that was likely to last forever. We grieved her loss because we felt she *was* lost; not only to us, but to herself.

The change happened all at once. She burst into the studio one night with dancing fires in her eyes as she told us she had to go out. She had a date.

Gwen hadn't had a date in several months, and had never shown any enthusiasm for the ones she'd had.

"I think we're onto something here," I said after she left. "It looks like true love, at last."

"Do you think it's a woman?"

"Who cares? Did you see her eyes? They were alive. When did you ever see her like that? Whoever it is, I hope it lasts."

"Even after being with me for all these years, you still think sex is the answer to everything."

"Dara, did you see her? Whatever it is, she needs more of it. And, for a twenty-four-year-old woman, finding someone *is* a big deal. I wouldn't be me if I hadn't fallen in love with you. A sizzling romance might be just the thing she needs– don't deny her the chance for her own experiences because you regret yours."

"She *was* sparkling." Dara seldom smiled when we talked about Gwen, but she was smiling now.

We hardly saw Gwen after that. She came home to Dara's to sleep and change clothes, but was never around long enough to supply the details that we were anxious to hear. I didn't see her for several weeks because she never came to the studio anymore. Dara reported that Gwen continued to look happy and energized. I was involved in a new painting, which consumed all my focus. The next time I saw Gwen, she was a different person.

She wouldn't tell us a thing about her new relationship except that it was a man, and that she wasn't ready for any of us to meet. In the past, Gwen had been very open with us. Now, she was secretive and circumspect. But happy.

Dara wanted to use the sheer force of her personality– a formidable weapon in any theater– to bully information from Gwen. Gwen's happiness, even if her enjoyment was just for the moment, was enough for me, and I suggested unobtrusive support. But, then, I wasn't Gwen's mother. Dara was unprepared to cede her will to mine in this disagreement. As a last resort, I petitioned for time and won that small skirmish.

Marcus. That was her boyfriend's name, and the only information she surrendered about him when she announced that she was going away with him for a week.

"Where are you going?" Dara asked.

"He hasn't told me. It's a surprise."

"And you're okay with that? That doesn't make you uneasy?"

"Why would it? I trust him completely. It's not like he's going to kidnap or hurt me, and we're way beyond rape. He's always surprising me, and the surprises are always nice."

"So why haven't we met him?"

"*Dara!*" I felt inclined to step in.

"That's okay, Leo. Marcus says he's not ready yet."

"Oh?" Dara's one word conveyed a complicated message to which Gwen wasn't receptive, and I didn't think she should pursue.

"*Dara!*"

"I was just asking. When, exactly, are you going?"

"Tomorrow. Isn't it wonderful?"

"Yeah, wonderful."

"What your mother means," I offered, "is that we hope you have a great time. Maybe, when you get back, you'll tell us all about it."

"Thanks, Leo. Mom, I'm not trying to be difficult. Marcus is kind of shy, in his way."

"Mothers worry, Gwen. Even super-hip mothers like me. Of course I want you to have a great time, and I'm so happy that you've found someone. I guess I'm jealous that I can't share any of it with you."

"This is just temporary. Marcus will come around. I think he's intimidated by you."

"Me? What have you told him?"

"Everything. Maybe I told him too much. He said we shouldn't have any secrets from each other. He's told me everything about himself."

"Such as?"

"*Dara!*"

"I'll tell you soon. I promise. Right now I'm going to go home to pack. We're leaving early in the morning. Gwen kissed us both good-bye and left. We didn't see her again until she returned from her trip.

Married.

Chapter 11

A week later, late on a Sunday night, Gwen called. Her voice was filled with electricity and a lilting happiness that I couldn't remember ever hearing before.

"Mom, Leo? It's Gwen. I'm in the Bahamas. I've got two really wonderful things to tell you."

"Hi, Gwen. You sound great. When are you coming back?"

"I don't know yet, Mom. But listen to my news."

"What is it?"

"Well, first of all, I won five hundred dollars at the casino last night."

A nice sum of money, but that, clearly, wasn't why she had called. She was much too happy for five hundred dollars.

"And the other thing . . . is that Marcus and I got married!"

Dara's gasp reached my ears both through the phone and from across the studio– it was that loud. She turned white and was trembling; holding the phone at arm's length and glowering at it as though it was evil. I didn't know whether to rush to Dara or to say something to Gwen.

"Gwen, are you still there? Dara didn't take your news very well. Is there a number where we can call you back?"

"This is a pay phone in the lobby. I don't know the hotel number."

"Call us back in fifteen minutes?"

"I'll try."

"I have to go see about your mother, uh, congratulations. Congratulate Marcus for me."

Dara was still staring at the phone, so drained of life and color that I expected her to crumble to the floor. I gently pushed her into a nearby chair and extricated the phone from her cold, sweaty grasp. then sat on the arm of the chair and rocked Dara while she cried.

Slowly, Dara pulled herself together. She didn't lose her composure often. In the years that we'd been together it did happen from time to time, but never lasted long. Dara's great strength was her self-assurance. I fed her tissue after tissue to absorb the flood until her breathing evened and the sickliness retreated from her body.

"That wasn't like me," she said when her composure took control. "The shock, and the unexpectedness, and the unanswered questions, and . . . my little girl is all of a sudden married, . . and I don't even . . ." her voice trailed off.

"Things will sort themselves out, Dara. Gwen's a good person and we have to trust her instincts. She's going to call back in a few minutes. Are you ready to talk to her?"

"Yes, of course. But *can* we trust her instincts? She's never dealt with impulses before. She's never had an impulse that I know of; she's certainly never acted impulsively. Along comes this guy who, incidentally, we know nothing about, sweeps her off her feet, and bam, they're married! Maybe he was just the first of several men with whom she was destined to fall in love. What if this is a huge mistake?"

"Why be pessimistic? She'll be calling back any minute, and we'll get more information. Then, when they come home, we'll all sit down and find out about Marcus. The situation can't be as bad as it seems right now."

"Leo, Gwen's married this Marcus person after knowing him for, what, two months? She's never ever even been on a third date with anyone. How can she have the judgment to decide to get married? And why has he avoided us? Especially if he was planning to marry her? Is he planning to never meet us? What *is* his problem, anyway?"

"I don't know. That part doesn't make any sense at all, but we can't do anything until we've talked to Gwen, talked to them both. She should have called by now."

Gwen never called back that night. The hour grew later and later until it was long past the time when Dara usually went home to get ready for the new work week. She was reluctant to leave, reluctant to be by herself. I offered to take her home and spend the night.

"I'd rather stay here, if it's okay with you."

"Like you have to ask. You look exhausted, anyway, and shouldn't drive. Why don't you go to bed, and I'll go get you some clothes for work tomorrow? Just tell me what you want."

"Don't bother. I'm not going to work tomorrow. Do you mind if I just stay here with you and watch you work?"

"I'll take the day off too, and we'll talk our faces off. Now, go to bed. I'll just close everything down for the night and be right there."

"You don't have to not-paint for me. I can't make you do that."

"We'll talk about it in the morning. Go to sleep."

"I love you, Leo."

"I know, and I love you, too."

Dara was asleep when I got into bed ten minutes later. At two in the morning, I was pretty tired myself after a long and disturbing day. I fell asleep as soon as my eyes closed.

And awoke a few hours later from a highly charged erotic dream only to discover that it wasn't a dream at all. Dara was naked and astride me with a feral look in her eyes and the scent of lust literally dripping from her sweat-coated body. We had been together for more than twelve years, and I had never experienced this side of her. At one time, I had hoped for this, but since it never came, I stopped anticipating a sexual revolution. Our lovemaking over the years had been more cerebral than physical, almost more of a psychic coupling than a physical one— intense but quiet, as though we'd spontaneously melted into one another.

There was nothing cerebral about what was happening at that moment. My initial concern for Dara— the way you'd be concerned if your loved one went on some sexual tear to avoid confronting more important problems— soon gave way to my innate maleness, so I stopped philosophizing and went for it. Dara was in a zone, and I was all too happy to join her there. The journey was exquisite.

We made love and slept in a pattern that continued until late the next afternoon when we were sore and swollen, and the room air was stale and rancid from our orgy. Although bed weary and ravenous, we were never happier, having crammed more sex into that one night than we'd had for the previous six months. That night was an awakening and a liberation for both of us.

We oozed our way into the shower, then sated our ravenous hunger with vanilla shakes at the local Dairy Queen because our lips and tongues were too sore and swollen for anything else. Not until we returned to the studio and moved into our favorite sofa with a bottle of wine, did we get into our postponed talk. Dara began.

"Before we get into Gwen, I want to talk about last night. What a self-centered, insensitive, priggish, psycho, asshole I've been all these years. Why you've stayed with me all this time, escapes me, but . . . thanks. I don't know how else to put it. Just, thanks. I love you so much, Leo. I guess it took the shock of Gwen's elopement to jolt me back to reality. Maybe part of my sexual repression had to do with not wanting Gwen to become what I was in college. Her marriage somehow freed me from all that."

"You don't have to apologize for yourself. I love the whole package. Whatever you do, whoever you are; it turns out that I love that. These last twenty-four hours have been a fantasy come true, but it doesn't change the way I feel about you. There's no way I can love you more than I already do."

We hugged and kissed and would have kissed longer, but our lips really were too sore. Instead, we sipped our wine– choosing its calming effect despite the burning.

"And now back to reality. What do we do about Gwen?" Dara asked.

"We don't know that we need to do anything. Maybe everything will be okay. Maybe this is for real. We all do stupid, dangerous things when we're young, and sometimes the results are okay. Sometimes, like for you, it takes years to get over them. Some people get completely fucked-over along the way, and for some, their impulsive acts turn out to be the best thing they could have done."

"But how do you know which one it's going to be?"

"That's irrelevant. You don't, and you don't have to. Gwen did this, and we have to let Gwen deal with it. Look at what happened between you and your mother. She must have been just as worried about you as you are about Gwen. Do you want Gwen to put you out of her life?"

"Even if you're right, what do I do in the meantime? How do I stop feeling this way?"

"You can start with more wine." I poured.

Three more days went by before we heard from Gwen. We had made some ineffectual attempts to contact her– we didn't know what hotel, which town, or whose name she was using. Feeling the need to do something, we continued to talk about it.

Gwen called me at my studio from Kennedy Airport on Thursday morning while Dara was at work. Fortunately, I had retained my old habit of leaving the answering machine on while I worked instead of shutting off the phone completely, and I heard her message.

There were only two people for whom I would stop painting and answer the phone: Dara and Mo. Neither one would interrupt me unless there was no choice. I answered Gwen's call for Dara, not for Gwen who, frankly, had pissed me off by the way she was handling her little escapade. She asked me to pick her up at the airport, but not even Dara would compel me to waste a morning of painting to make the two-hour round trip, so I paid for an airport van to bring her to Northport.

Dara was in a conference when I called, but managed to get to the studio just before Gwen arrived. Gwen looked tired but happy. She hugged us both as we looked around her for the elusive Marcus. He wasn't there.

"Where's Marcus?"

"He had business out west, so he went on to San Diego from the airport."

"Gwen, there *is* a Marcus, right?"

"Of course, Mom," she laughed, tentatively. "He'll be back soon. And he wants to meet you now."

"How friendly of him!" The sarcasm was waist deep. Gwen didn't seem to notice. Or if she did, she didn't care.

Dara extracted some information from Gwen. Marcus was some kind of traveling point man for a Wall Street brokerage firm. He was twenty-three, from New York, and had gone to college in Tulsa. His father owned his own business, and his mother was a housewife. Gwen thought they were rich. Marcus was somewhat estranged from his family– there was no incident or hostility, but they weren't high on his priority list. Oh yes, and he loved children– the more, the better– and dogs– the larger, the better– and Gwen, just the way she was.

Marcus was expected back in a week or two. The newlyweds planned to stay at Marcus' studio apartment in Queens until they found a larger place for themselves. Gwen asked if she could stay at Dara's until Marcus returned because she didn't think she'd be comfortable at Marcus' alone and, besides, he hadn't given her the keys.

"Doesn't he trust you?"

"It was just an oversight. We were so rushed at the airport that Marcus almost missed his plane. And I didn't think to ask."

"Are you hungry? Can I get you anything?"

"No, just tired. It's been a whirlwind two weeks. I just need a nap."

"Well, you can nap here or take my car and go home. I'm going to sleep here tonight, so I don't need my car until the morning."

Dara and I had spent every night together since Sunday– a kind of honeymoon for us.

"And Gwen, our house is your house and always will be. I'm sure, without asking, that Leo will always welcome you here, too.

Don't ever think you need to ask to come home. Go get some sleep and we'll regroup later."

After Gwen left, Dara sat quietly for a while, deep in thought.

"You'd never have done that, you know?"

"Done what?"

"Gone off and left your new bride to fend for herself; get back from the airport, find a place to stay, deal with me, everything. And while we're at it, you would never have married Gwen without meeting her family."

"Don't forget, you met me when I was over forty and already established in my profession. Things might have been very different if you had met me before *Schoolbuses*. And even now, if I was in the middle of a painting, I *might* let you fend for yourself."

"Not you. Not to me. And that's what I'm talking about. Why isn't Gwen as important to Marcus as I am to you? This is from a man who had to rush into marriage because his love was so urgent."

"Maybe it's all circumstantial. What if I were in a fugue when you needed me? Who'd do the fending then?"

"That's hardly the same because you have no control over that. He could have ended the honeymoon one day earlier to make sure that Gwen was okay. Gwen doesn't seem to care, but I haven't even met him and I'm already uneasy.".

Two weeks later, I received a package addressed to me at my studio with no return address. Inside was a set of house keys which, I assumed, belonged to Marcus.

Chapter 12

Gwen recognized the keys. She didn't comment on the peculiar way they were sent to her, nor that she hadn't, otherwise, heard from Marcus. Just in case she hadn't noticed, Dara brought it to her attention. Gwen remained unfazed.

"Marcus is always doing unexpected things. He loves to keep me guessing. It's very romantic. He told me that he might be too busy working to call me all the time. This probably means that he'll be coming home soon. I should be there when he does."

"Gwen, you've been married for, what, less than a month? And your newlywed husband couldn't find a few minutes in his busy schedule to call you?"

"Marcus is so intense when he's working. You know what that's like, Leo? You know how you get when you're painting? Marcus is like that, too. Wait till you meet him, Mom. I know you're going to love him."

"Just tell me when you want to go to Queens. I'll drive you."

"As soon as you can, if you don't mind."

"Don't you need time to pack up your things?"

"Oh, I'm not going to take much. Marcus doesn't like my clothes, and doesn't want me to wear them. Marcus is going to buy me new clothes when he gets back." The smoke coming from Dara's ears was only partially obscured by the fire coming out of her nostrils.

"What's wrong with the clothes you have now?"

"They're too young and flashy. I'm married now. I need to settle down."

"Settle down from what?" I finally had to interject. Gwen wore jeans and sweat shirts. Hardly *flashy*. The conversation was too bizarre to ignore. "Is this you talking, or is this Marcus?"

"Well, Marcus says that I represent him now, and the way I look and act reflects on him. In the corporate world, he's constantly being scrutinized."

"That's all I needed to know," I said. There was nothing to say. I had lived through draft card burning, and flag burning, and bra burning. You didn't have to be Gloria Steinhem to know this was wrong, wrong, WRONG. How could I even begin to explain that to Gwen if she didn't already know it? Dara, however, was just warming to the conflict. Her eyes were sharp and focused, her body coiled. Her voice was level and clear. She was ready to pounce.

"And you're going to let him do this to you? You're twenty-four. Your life is just beginning. There are a million things for you to try for the first time. A million moments to experience. Why would you possibly want to "settle down?" This should be a time when you and Marcus are exploring the universe and each other. To hell with the corporate world!"

"You *are* the corporate world, Mom. It's easy for you to say fuck-you to the corporate world because you've got Leo with all his money. Marcus is just starting out and doesn't have a famous artist to support him. And don't you and Leo make compromises for each other? Hah, I see you do it all the time."

"Leo would never ask me to subordinate my needs to his. When we compromise for each other, it's exactly that. I do it for Leo because I love him. He does it for me because he loves me. We would never demand anything from each other."

"You're making too much of this. I don't have any special attachment to my old clothes. Aren't they just as much your taste as they are mine? So what's the difference if it's your taste or Marcus'?"

"You're missing the point."

"That's because you're not making one. What I'm doing is far worse. I'm disagreeing with the great and mighty Dara Harrington!"

The time had come to step in despite the risk of getting them both angry at me. I didn't care about Gwen, but Dara and I had been in a special place, and I wasn't ready to leave it yet. Dara was getting more and more upset, and she was capable of letting her wrath get in the way of good sense. Dara still didn't speak to her own mother after twenty-five years. If she was poised to issue an intractable ultimatum, Gwen might run off, and be left with no one to turn to if she needed help.

"Gwen, why don't you go back to Dara's . . . that is, go back *home* and get whatever you need? Then come back here, and we'll both drive you to Queens."

Gwen took the keys and ducked out. Dara glowered at her retreating figure. She glowered at the door. She glowered at the ceiling. She glowered at me.

"You're glowering."

"I know I'm glowering. I want to glower. I need to glower. Are you ready to stop telling me everything will be okay? Or are you going to continue to delude yourself and try to delude me?"

"No, it's time to start worrying. Don't be angry at me just because you turned out to be right. Though it sure doesn't look good at the moment. it didn't necessarily have to play out like this. Maybe this is just one issue and they'll be okay about everything else."

"Do you really believe that?"

"No."

"If only she had acknowledged that there was something wrong and chose to ignore it. But she doesn't even see it. How can she protect herself if she doesn't even see it? What kind of a weasel is this Marcus?"

"You've got to let it go for now, Dara. If you alienate her, you won't be there to help her if she needs you. Then what?"

"You're right. I'll try."

We drove Gwen to Forest Hills and departed on good terms. She didn't give us her new phone number. She had "forgotten" it.

Chapter 13

Despite my advice to Dara about judging Marcus too soon, his behavior left me with an uneasy feeling. Gwen's reference to my money concerned me–. concerned me that Marcus might somehow try to get the money from the trust that I had set up for Gwen. Making the leap from Gwen's hurried marriage and unexplained secrecy to concern for my worldly possessions was paranoid thinking. There was no money in Gwen's trust yet, and there wouldn't be until my death. Most of the rest of my estate would go to Dara, and therefore, eventually, to Gwen as well. Since I wasn't planning to die soon, the relationship between Marcus and Gwen should be sorted out by the time Gwen had access to anything. The logic wasn't enough to allay my fears. Whenever money issues arise, Mo has always been my best advisor.

Mo's daughter found him for me, awash on a beach in Honolulu. I hadn't spoken to Mo in several months so it was both heartwarming and reassuring to hear his voice.

"And this Marcus, does he have a last name?"

"Davis."

"That doesn't help. I know a million Davises. What company does he work for? We should call them."

"I'm ashamed to say that I don't know. We haven't even met him yet, and Gwen keeps all information about him pretty close to her vest."

"Leo, I'm eight thousand miles away and this may be none of my business– and I don't want to alarm you– but this stinks. There's too much secrecy going on, and in a situation where secrecy shouldn't matter. It's almost like he's trying to be a shadowy figure. Why would he want that?"

"Dara is going crazy with all this. As for you, my business has always been your business. Any help or advice would be greatly appreciated."

"Call Lee and tell her I said to call around on Wall Street and see if we can find out where he's working. Then you can call the personnel director and at least get a background check. Tell them who you are and that this kid approached you with an investment offer, using their company as his reference. They'll talk to you. Let me run this by Barbara and think about it a little. I'll get back to you."

Barbara had been right. Mo's reluctance to retire soon gave way to the enjoyment of freedom and travel. Lee was bringing the gallery into the twenty-first century without ceding an ounce of its bygone glory.

"This whole thing troubles me in more ways than one. I don't like to feel so mercenary, but my first reaction was to protect my money. "

"Haven't I taught you anything? It never hurts to prepare for the worst, even if you never need it."

"Thanks for calling Mo. I don't want to keep you away from the Mai Tais and the bikinis for too long."

*   *   *

Marcus worked for one of the well-known and reputable Wall Street firms. His job was to scout small communities to evaluate the feasibility of opening a branch office– no sales responsibilities and no personal clients. Although he was on a list for aspiring brokers, he had chosen not to take the in-house preparatory course, opting instead for the alternative, and far less likely road of working in less attractive jobs while hoping to attract someone's attention.

The director of personnel, confirmed that Marcus had attended Oral Roberts University, but added that he'd left after two years. Marcus had been hired by his predecessor, so the personnel director never actually met Marcus, and couldn't offer any additional personal information. .

Had anyone ever met Marcus?

We didn't hear from Gwen for another month until she called me at my studio in the middle of the day. Once again, I picked up the phone for Dara's sake, who wouldn't want to let the call slip by. Although Dara and I were continuing in our new lover/honeymoon relationship, all our talk was about Gwen and the elusive Marcus. My voice reflected my annoyance– for both the interruption and the way Gwen was conducting her married life.

"Hi, Leo, it's Gwen. Sorry to keep bothering you at work."

"I'll talk to you, Gwen, but on one condition."

"There's always *one condition* with you and Mom. What is it now?"

"Before we talk, you have to give me a number where Dara can reach you."

Silence.

"Gwen, she's your mother."

"Uh . . . okay . . . but only in an emergency."

"Excuse me?"

"Marcus doesn't want me to tie up the line."

"And which of the dozens of intimate friends you've made does that?"

"It's just that Marcus does a lot of business over the phone. He doesn't want to miss a call from a client who needs him."

"Gwen, you're scaring me. Marcus won't let your mother call you occasionally?"

"He's kind of set in his ways."

"How about this? Will you let me send you a cell-phone in my name so you can call Dara from time to time? You can keep it with you and you don't have to even call from home."

"Not right now, Leo. Maybe later. Besides, I don't go out much."

I had known Gwen for a long time, from girl to woman, but I had never seen her act scared, and she sounded scared right then. Her tone softened me

"Gwen, are you all right?"

"Sure, Leo."

"If you want out, just say the word. We'll send in the cavalry."

"However it sounds to you, it's not like that at all. Marcus is very good to me. He's very attentive, and we're both very much in love.

"Okay. You still haven't told me why you called me and not your mother."

"To ask for your help."

"With what?"

"Breaking the news."

"Which is?"

"Marcus and I are going to have a baby!"

Silence.

Silence.

Finally, I broke it.

"What?"

"Please be happy for me, Leo. I'm so happy!"

"That's because you're so crazy!"

"I was hoping that *you* would understand. That's why I told you first."

"Gwen, you just got married to a guy you've only known for a short time. He's never home and whether you want to admit it or not, he sounds like a control freak. Why can't you give this some time to see if it works out? You've got a whole life in which to have babies."

"It's too late. I'm over two months pregnant. It happened on the honeymoon."

"Oh, good! That was responsible. And when is Marcus going to deign to meet your parents?"

"I don't have "parents," Leo, just a mother. And that should be between us."

That hurt. It hurt a lot. I would have to think about that later. Right now, I was a representative-of-Dara's-best-interests, and not a separate entity. My own emotional health would have to wait.

"And yet you called me for help?" Her actions had belied her words, but that didn't help. "What exactly is our relationship, then?" My voice struggled to remain calm.

"Are you going to help me or not?"

"You'll never get Dara's blessing until and unless she meets Marcus. There are certain things I feel confident in saying for Dara, and that is definitely one of them."

"Marcus would agree to meet Dara in some neutral place, but he doesn't want to meet you. He says that he's the man in my life now, and that should be enough."

"Yeah, okay (it wasn't). I'll tell Dara your news, but she's going to want to speak to you immediately when she hears it. I won't tell her if she can't."

"I'll call her at ten tonight."

"Give me your number or I won't tell her."

"I'll call back at ten."

Click.

Chapter 14

Dara called at 7:30. She was still at work trying to wrap up a difficult day. If she ever did get finished, she was planning to go right home and crawl into bed because the next day wasn't looking any better.

"You sound exhausted, but Gwen's going to call you here at ten, and you're going to want to talk to her. I could tell her to call you at home, but will she?'

"I'll be there. I sleep better there with you, anyway. What's it about?"

"Not over the phone. Let's not get into one of those you-brought-it-up-now-you-have-to-tell-me discussions. Concentrate on finishing what you're doing, and we'll talk later."

"Okay, I won't be much longer. I'm running out of brain cells. Do we have any salad stuff left?"

"There will be a delicious salad and a hot bath waiting for you when you get here. See you soon."

When Dara arrived, she looked as exhausted and frazzled as she had said. I just held her for a while, hoping to transfer some energy from my body to hers. She wasn't going to like Gwen's news, and if Gwen was really going to call at ten– and how likely was that?– she needed to know and have the strength to deal with her daughter in an appropriate manner. She briefly picked a the waiting salad, then I practically had to carry her to the bathroom where I helped her into a hot bubble bath.

Easing her into the bath was like attending to a child who had fallen asleep in the car on the way home. She was limp as I took off her clothes and got her into the water. Sitting on the side of the tub I distractedly swirled the water with my hand. When I looked up, Dara's head was back against the porcelain rim of the tub and she was sound asleep.

After preparing a pot of strong but decaffeinated coffee– to get her awake enough to talk, but not enough to keep her up all night, I waved a cup of it under Dara's nose to awaken her, alternately caressing her inner thigh and her neck with my other hand. Dara liked to be awakened gently and loud noises or shaking always put her in a bad mood. It wasn't working.

What to do next? She looked like she really needed to sleep, but she couldn't spend the night in the tub no matter whether Gwen called, or not. Slipping my hands under her arms, I pulled her forward toward me. Dara opened her eyes and gave me a weak smile as she folded her arms around my neck.

"Dara, Dara. You've got to get out of the tub. Come to bed." Dara stepped out of the tub and stood quietly as I wrapped a towel around her, then she came to life.

"I'm awake now. We've got to talk. Do I smell coffee?"

"Yeah, I made a pot. Let's get you into bed and we'll have some, and talk."

"No, I'll fall asleep in bed. Let's go sit on the couch."

Now that she was awake and listening, I relayed my conversation with Gwen.

"Shit! What a little bitch.. She said that to you? To *you*! You must feel awful."

"Believe me, Dara, the last thing I feel like doing right now is defending Gwen, but she's being manipulated by Marcus.. That wasn't Gwen on the phone this afternoon, that was him. Gwen sounded scared. Scared. Married, pregnant and scared. Have you ever seen Gwen scared?"

"Not even as a little girl. I'm scared now, too. What can we do?"

"The first thing we have to do is meet him. Maybe it's all Gwen's problem. If it is, and Marcus is a reasonable person, we can get her some help. If he's as bad as we think he is, we're going to need a lot of help. We should call Dr. Jamison and see what she thinks."

"I'm too tired to think logically, right now. My mind is churning, all I can think about is the immediate problem. Gwen could be in serious trouble!"

"It's nine forty-five, she should be calling very soon, and maybe we'll get some answers."

"Though it seems unlikely, just in case I fall asleep, make sure you wake me. Shake me, punch me, pour hot coffee over my head. Whatever it takes."

After an hour, Dana laid back on the bed. Her tossing and turning made it unclear whether she was awake or asleep, but I didn't want to disturb her. At midnight, extremely tired myself from the emotional toll of the day, I climbed into bed beside her.

Gwen never called that night.

Chapter 15

Leo Schultz. Yeah, that's me. The original macho man. Defender of the hearth. Champion of my loved ones. Pillar of strength in times of crisis. Laugher in the face of doom. Dependable and resourceful. That's me. I was a big help.

I fugued.

Years had passed since my last fugue, so many years that they were no longer a part of my concern, and I seldom thought about them anymore. I was no longer doing Cubism or Still Lifes, or Surrealism or anything else. I was doing Leo Schultz.

"Shit," is the thought that would have come to mind if I had been capable of thinking. Nevertheless, I fugued.

The fugue lasted two weeks. A long one. But after fourteen days, reinvigorated and tremendously clearheaded, I was ready to take on any dragon stupid enough to mess with me. There were two major differences with that fugue. First, when I woke up, Dara was sleeping beside me. She had never had the temerity to do that before. There was the lurking element of danger, and the total lack of control of the situation was spooky and upsetting to her. None of my girlfriends from college, nor Sylvie, Ellen, nor anyone else had ever been beside me when I reawakened.

My clock radio read *9:00 A.M.*, but the alarm wasn't set; so it was likely to be a weekend morning. I rolled over to face Dara and put my arm across her, pulling her toward me, loving the fact that she was there.

Dara woke up and looked surprised to see me.

"That's it?"

"I just woke up."

"Just like that?"

"No, first I howled at the moon for a few minutes and then the hairy parts gradually turned back to skin and the claws retracted. See (I held up my hands) back to normal."

"Whoa. Back off. This is my first time. I guess I expected some sort of transition. One minute you're Sleeping Beauty and the next minute you're Leo."

"Yeah, that's the magic. And the scary part. How come you're here? Is everything okay with Gwen?"

"I don't know. Gwen still hasn't called. I'm here because I missed you, and wanted to be with you even if you *were* a lump. You've been gone for two weeks, by the way, leaving me frustrated and miserable all that time. I've sent messengers to Gwen and I've sent telegrams. Nothing."

"I've let you down."

"Just because it's been years, don't go back to apologizing. You have no control over your fugues. I wasn't faulting you. Last night, I needed to be close to you even if you couldn't be close back, so I came over. There was nothing to miss on the Gwen front."

"But I could have been around for you."

"As it turns out, you were. I don't know if I'm more worried for Gwen or angry with her for what she's doing to herself . . . and I haven't even touched on what she told you. *I don't have parents, just a mother"* Dara imitated Gwen's voice in a mocking tone.

"Let's have some breakfast and drive to Gwen's. What the hell? We have nothing to lose."

"Don't you have some Japanese brush painting or something you have to paint and *now*?"

"No . . . not really. Whatever it is, it can wait."

That was the other thing.

The fugues were a major cause of embarrassment to me as a child and teenager, but no more than that. They set me apart from other children; made me weirder, more fragile, but they weren't a physical presence between episodes. Nor did they interfere with my plans because they never came at a crucial time. The feeling of total refreshment and well-being that followed more than compensated for the inconvenience.

The change from photorealism to abstract expressionism that occurred several months after *Schoolbuses*, was a concern, but didn't destroy my newly-blossoming career.

After the next show, and my continued success, the fugues were adventures, marred only by their unpredictabhility. If it wasn't for that, and the social awkwardness when I had to explain my absences, I would have looked forward to them. Certainly, there had been fugues I could have skipped– such as the Christmas week when Ellen and I were teetering on the edge of oblivion– but I had never been irrevocably affected by a fugue.

In the last few years, when the fugues were infrequent, I looked forward to them as a kind of vacation. There was no place in the world where you could go for a week or ten days and come back feeling the way I did after a fugue. The desire to take my painting in a new direction, and the million new ideas that I couldn't wait to get onto a canvas were added pluses. Until now.

Although I felt great and was overflowing with energy, there were no new paintings, no new passion. And my old ideas, the unfinished canvases in my studio, seemed tepid and banal. There was nothing I wanted to paint.

Before *Schoolbuses*, I had frustratingly searched for my personal artistic perspective unable to get obsessed about my paintings, yet still obsessed with painting. I threw away every last one of my early attempts, but I was still a painter, painting is what I did. Painting is always what I've done. There was no separation between Leo Schultz the man, and Leo Schultz the painter. Until now.

Until now! Painting didn't interest me. No matter what I did, or how hard I tried to make the feeling return, the desire to paint had vanished. Dara listened to my words of frustration for hours. We spent as much time on Leo Shultz's problem as we did on Gwen's. Mo called me daily from all over the globe. We all agreed on the platitudes that just begged to be chosen: *It will pass, don't push it, take a little mental vacation, don't think about it and it will happen.*

The bad part– which makes the good part consist of the misery of not being able to paint and how that made me feel about myself– was that I had nothing else to do except concentrate on Gwen.

I didn't know it then, but my total absorption with Gwen began on the car ride from Northport to Queens. We left home in the late afternoon, thinking that Gwen and Marcus were most likely to be home in the early evening. Dara and I were like a perpetual motion machine, each fueling the other's concern and wrath, going over every detail– though the hard facts were scant– from when Gwen had her first "date" with Marcus, until the very moment we were speeding down the Long Island Expressway toward Gwen's apartment in Forest Hills.

By the time we arrived, and after two hours spent reinforcing each other's misgivings, we were both frantic about Gwen's plight and belligerent in anticipation of Marcus trying to stop us from seeing her.. Not being able to find a parking spot near Gwen's apartment– all the street spaces and all of the parking lots were full– added fuel to our outrage. After circling the block four or five times, and still fuming over Gwen's predicament, we left the car parked at a fire hydrant praying for a ticket rather than being towed.

Dara pushed the intercom button.

"Who is it?" Gwen's voice.

"It's me, Mom. Let us up."

"This isn't a good time. You should have called." She sounded terrified.

"If I could have called, I wouldn't have had to come. Let us in."

Silence. We realized she was no longer listening. Dara rang again. Marcus answered this time.

"Please go away. Gwen told you it was a bad time. She'll call you soon."

"We want to see her, now." He wasn't listening either.

We stood in the entranceway deciding what to do next. A tenant entered the building, eyeing us suspiciously. We looked maniacal and capable of just about any heinous crime. The woman never took her eyes off of us as she let herself into the building. I surprised both her and myself– probably myself more since she was expecting me to do something criminal– by bursting through the door after her, and calling Dara to follow me, trying to look extremely normal and under control as I turned to the screaming woman and said, "I know you're upset. The right thing for you to do is call the police and tell them to meet us at apartment 12E."

When we ran to the elevators and pushed the button, the doors opened immediately. The woman chose not to get on with us. We got off at the twelfth floor and ran in two directions until Dara called to me from in front of Gwen's apartment. She rang the bell.

There was no answer and no answer, still, after several more rings. We pounded on the door. Still nothing.

"Come on, Gwen, open the door. We're not going to stay. Just talk to us for one minute (still banging)."

Finally, Marcus spoke.

"Go away. We told you that this wasn't a good time. We'll call you, soon."

"What are you afraid of, Marcus? We just want to meet you and see Gwen. That's all."

"Go away, Mr. Schultz, you're not part of this. If you don't leave now, I'm going to call the police."

"We've already called them. They should be here any time now."

"And what are you going to tell them? That the tenants in 12E won't let you break into their apartment? Have fun."

There was no more talking from inside the apartment. We continued to pound on the door, but with significantly less commitment. The elevator doors opened and a policeman and our friend from the lobby got out. She nodded in our direction.

"That's them."

"Thank you, ma'am. You'll be safer back in your own apartment. I'll talk to you later." He pulled his gun and pointed it at us.

"Step away from each other and put both of your hands on top of your heads."

90

"I can explain, officer," I said as I turned toward him.

"Freeze! (I did), now do as I said (I did)." He patted us down, although quite gingerly with Dara. Then said, "Now you can talk."

"Can I turn around?"

"Slowly."

"My name is Leo Schultz and this is Dara Harrington. Dara's daughter, Gwen, is in this apartment. In the space of three months, Gwen has met the man in there, married him and gotten pregnant. She won't give us her phone number, and we still haven't met him. We're just two very concerned parents and we're not bad people, just desperate. Are you a father?"

"Yeah."

"Well, then you've gotta understand."

"Do you have an I.D.?"

"Yes, of course." I reached for my wallet.

"Slowly."

"Are you the girl's father?" he said, with one eye fixed on me while he tried to read my license with the other.

"Not technically. Dara is Gwen's mother, and we've all been together for twelve years. I feel like her father, but I'm not."

"Can I see your I.D. ma'am?" He looked at it for a long time, but, of course, nothing on it was of any help to the situation. "I'm going to have to take you down to the precinct to talk to my lieutenant."

Oh, great! Now on top of everything else, we were going to be arrested. Arrest and tedious questions were not what I wanted. I wanted the policeman to make Marcus open the door. Unfortunately, he was in charge.

"Er, officer, there may be one more little problem. When we got here, we couldn't find a parking spot, and we were in such a hurry that I left the car next to a hydrant."

The policeman did not look pleased. "Okay," he said at last, "you come with me, and the lady can follow us in your car."

We spent the next three hours explaining ourselves to the lieutenant. Mo was somewhere out of the country, and the answering machine picked up at my lawyer's office. Lee couldn't provide more than a bodyless voice, a voice that could have belonged to anyone, volunteering a character reference. Marcus had the law on his side. He had committed no crime– although Dara had a long list of the crimes she thought he had committed– and done nothing wrong. We filled out and signed more official-looking forms than I would have thought necessary. Finally, they let us go after one last stern lecture by the lieutenant.

"That was a productive and in no way humiliating experience. Can I show a girl a fun evening or what?"

"You were perfect, Leo. You did exactly what was needed to be done."

"But nothing *got* done!"

"Nothing got done about Gwen. But I feel much better. Right now, that's enough."

"It seemed like such a good idea at the time."

"The only thing that would make this night any better would be the sudden appearance of a diner on the horizon. I'm starving."

"If you can't find a twenty-four-hour diner on Queen's Boulevard, where can you find one?"

We settled for a coffee shop, which smelled bad, and served awful-tasting food, but we didn't care. Dara was playful, almost euphoric. Our trip to Gwen's apartment, though a total failure, had inexplicably buoyed her mood.

But it was short lived– our euphoria and our hunger dissipated at the same time. We sipped at lukewarm, watered-down, decaffeinated coffee, and I pushed a couple of pieces of toast around my plate while Dara hardly looked at her sandwich. We left after just a few minutes and rode home in silence as each of us pursued our own, morbid thoughts. As we approached Northport, Dara broke the silence.

"I'd like to sleep at my place tonight, if it's okay with you."

"With or without me?"

"With. I don't ever want to sleep without you again. Is that okay?"

"Dara." I barely got her name out of my throat. After weeks of emotional beating for both of us, that night, though awful and depressing, was also bringing Dara and me closer together—something we would have thought impossible just a few months before. I wanted to tell Dara how much I loved her, but I was too choked up to speak coherently.

Nor could I drive. Pulling the car to the shoulder of the road and reaching for Dara, we hugged and we kissed with tears streaming down both of our faces.

The release of all that emotion was so intense that we were unaware of the car that pulled in behind us, until a State Trooper shined his flashlight on us. He rapped on the window with the heel of his flashlight. Dara opened her window.

"Are you folks okay?"

Stopping to blow my nose, I used the time to think of what to say. For two basically law abiding citizens, Dara and I were facing our second encounter with the police that night.

"Yes, officer. We both got very emotional about our daughter, and I thought it would be safest to pull over for a minute instead of driving."

"Well, the shoulder of this road isn't the safest place. But I've got a reckless son myself, so I understand. Do you think you're okay to drive now?"

"Yes."

"Be careful pulling onto the highway. Take care, now."

"Thank you, sir." We left.

The policeman followed us until we exited, four miles later. He either wanted to make sure we were okay or to find out if I was drunk. Either way, we made it to Dara's without incident.

Usually, Dara and I slept together at my house. When I was painting, it was where we spent the most time. We hadn't slept at Dara's since the onset of our new sexual relationship. That night, however, we were both too exhausted to make love, so just held each other for a few minutes before falling asleep.

At seven-thirty the next morning, my feelings about Gwen were neutral, and the greatest proportion of my thoughts were about Dara. But Dara wasn't beside me in bed– she wasn't anywhere in the house. Curious, but not concerned, there was nothing to do except wait for her to show up or call, so I made coffee and showered. While halfway through my second cup of coffee, Dara returned in running clothes, out of breath and sweaty. She slumped into a chair next to me, and I got up to get her a cup of coffee.

On my way to the pot it occurred to me that she might not want hot coffee."

"Do you want coffee?"

"Yes, but ice-water first, please."

I got her the ice-water and pulled a wad of paper towels off the roll. Dara sipped the water as I wiped her face and neck, and then pulled off her wet T-shirt and dried her upper body as best as I could, though she continued to sweat.

"Thanks, Leo."

"Where were you?"

"Out running."

"Dara, you don't run."

"I needed to, today. I had a lot of pent up energy and didn't want to wake you. It felt good."

Dara showered and came back to the kitchen, where we quickly got back to the subject of Gwen.

"How could this have happened? One minute Gwen was our pet rock, and the next minute she's married, pregnant and completely out of our lives. We thought we had a problem when she didn't do anything. Should we have seen this coming?"

"Even Dr. Jamison was surprised. Don't beat yourself, Dara, you've been a good mother. Even all those years you were alone, Gwen was always your priority. Why this happened, who knows? You can't predict everything– how can you tell what's going to shape a personality until it's shaped? You're worried about Gwen and so am I. Last night was the limit of my ideas, short of hiring one of those de-programmers to kidnap her and stay with her in a locked room until she is back to reality."

"That won't work. We're going to lose her, anyway. I know how it works. Once you split, it's impossible to go back. I've been there. This is another case of the curse of the parents being visited on the children."

"So, then, what?"

"We should go see see someone we can talk to about Gwen. If we can't help her, maybe, at least, we'll get advice about what to do for ourselves."

"I'll get the yellow pages. How do I look this up? We don't even know what to call it."

"Dr. Jamison gave me some names; they're on my desk."

The earliest appointment we could get was for the end of the next week. Determined not to think about Gwen in the interim, we stopped talking about her, but continued to brood in silence.

Three days before our appointment, Gwen called.

Chapter 16

Her voice rang with a thick layer of carefree good will applied over her sadness with a pallette knife. Gwen would visit Dara, but I was still to be exiled from her life. Marcus was going away for two weeks and he had *given his permission* for Gwen to come to Dara's for the weekend. In fact, he had insisted on it.

She was coming by train on Friday morning and would remain until Sunday night. Marcus didn't think she should stay longer.

The visit gave us a focus for our first meeting with Dr. Rosenthal, the psychologist we had selected. We were scheduled to see him on the day before Gwen's arrival. Even though Gwen had excluded me, Dara was excited about seeing her daughter. Our only concern was, that like all the times she had promised to phone, Gwen wouldn't show up.

Dr. Rosenthal was the kind of therapist everyone dreams of having. The aura he generated was so reassuring that it promised that if he just hugged me, and told me that everything would be okay, it would. With his professorial demeanor and a twinkle in his eye, he seemed unflappable.

We gave him as detailed a history as we could, which he followed with a lot of questions about how Gwen had reacted to specific incidents during her adolescence. The information he received in a letter from Dr. Jamison supplemented what we told him with her psychological evaluation.. The doctor reacted like he had heard Gwen's type of story many times before.

He also spent a lot of time asking me about my fugues. That surprised me because there didn't seem to be any connection between my fugues and Gwen's married life.

"And you feel nothing during all this time?"

"It's like sleep without dreaming– very quiet, the faintest sensation of swirling lights, otherwise, nothing."

"I've never heard of this before. Someone should write a paper about you. The creative energy you acquire from those episodes is what intrigues me the most. I know your work; I have a lithograph of *Seraglio* (one of my paintings from the same series as *Junction*) hanging in my bedroom. It is so beautiful, but dark and cryptic." I didn't want to think about what a trained psychiatrist could deduce about me from *Seraglio*.

"Right now, my waking life concerns me more than my fugue states."

"You're right, Leo, that's not why you came. Dara, let me get back to you "

He interviewed Dara about all aspects of Gwen's life, and some more about how she'd dealt with Gwen over certain issues in the past.

When we were done, he sat pensively for a few seconds and said, "These situations can't be dealt with using one pat formula. Why don't you help yourselves to some coffee over there while I take a few minutes to think about this?" After just a few minutes, he was ready.

"There are really two issues here: How to deal with Gwen when she comes to visit this weekend, and how to make her realize what she's letting Marcus do to her? The first is more imminent and, happily, easier to handle. I'll have a better idea of how to proceed with the second issue once I have the information that you, Dara, will get this weekend. It's very important that you get as much information as you can. Browbeating or being judgmental isn't going to work. Will you work with me?"

"Of course, anything."

"And you, Leo? Can you stay away all weekend, even if Dara calls for help?"

"Yes, as long as she's not in any danger."

"Good. Now Dara, if you ask Gwen how she's doing, she'll most likely say *fine,* or some other meaningless answer, and the conversation is over. The first thing for you to do is remind her, with actions, not words, how things were when she lived with you. How people treated each other and so on. If the two of you had a favorite thing you used to do together, no matter how far back you have to go, try to do it.

"Get her into a state of warm, cozy relaxation. Let her feel how good it feels to feel good, and safe, and loved. Hug and stroke her a lot– even to the point where you think you're overdoing it.

"Maybe that's all you'll accomplish this time. That's okay. It will just make her want to come back.

"You can also say things like. *This feels so good; it brings me back to when you were a little girl.* This may make her want to talk, but whatever you do, don't push. Promise me that the strongest words you'll say will be something like *we've noticed a change in you.* Can you do that?"

"I'll try my best. Sometimes, though, I get so infuriated at that bastard, Marcus."

"Just concentrate on what's best for Gwen, and you'll do fine. Your job is to get Gwen out of there. Let dealing with Marcus be someone else's problem. The authorities. Or God."

We left Dr. Rosenthal's office feeling much better, and more in control. Our next appointment was in two weeks.

Dara took off from work on Friday to spend the day with Gwen. Still riding the optimism derived from Dr. Rosenthal's aura, we were certain that Gwen would show up. Since I wasn't part of this scenario, I went into the City to nose around my former haunts.

My first stop was at Mo's, which was now, more accurately, Lee's gallery. Lee was preparing for a new show of young, inner-city artists. She had a good eye and the artists she had selected were all talented. We talked for a while, but she was very busy and needed to get back to work.

I visited my old Village hang-outs. To my dismay, the familiar coffee houses and bars where artists congregated to share ideas and gossip were either closed, gone upscale, or catering to a whole different clientele. The only artist I ran across was Gordon Sculler, the washed-up comic strip creator who had, years ago, traded success for alcohol.

Desperate to make a connection, no matter how marginal an artist he was, I bought Gordon a drink. Fueled with another scotch, the old-timer became expansive, ruing the loss of the sense of community, as much, I thought, for the diminished supply of free drinks, as for true philosophical angst. If I wanted to find anyone, Gordon told me, my best bet was the New School where several older artists were now teaching courses.

When I left him, disheartened and like a stranger in what had been my own neighborhood for twenty years, I intended to walk down to Soho, look into some of the galleries, then go home. Gordon had referred to my peers as the *older artists*. That might have been enough of a lesson to learn, for one day. Though in my own mind, I was just getting started, the irony was that I hadn't painted a stroke in several months.

Fifteen minutes later, without planning it, I found myself standing in front of the New School. Many of the names on the Art faculty list were familiar to me. One of them, Joe Bernington, was in his office.

"Leo Shultz! What brings you back to the City? I thought you were in hiding out on Long Island somewhere, like Rivers and Sandusky. Come, sit down, I'm glad you stopped by." Joe greeted me like a close friend when, in fact, we had been only casual acquaintances.

"I tell you, Leo, as much as I loved to paint, watching these young kids develop their talent gives me a tremendous rush. When I can help them pull things together, I get a sense of accomplishment I never got from my own canvasses."

Joe had been a good technical painter with a good feeling for color, but had never been more than moderately successful. His paintings had been too safe, and we had lived in radical times. Joe appeared to have found his niche. His excitement and interest in his students made him an excellent teacher and he was well liked and respected by his students.

Though my drink with Gordon had been depressing, and that mood had lasted all the way into his office, I liked Joe and enjoyed his company. We filled each other in on the past few years, except that I neglected to mention my recent inability to paint.

"Have you ever considered teaching, Leo?"

"No, because I have a problem with the concept of *teaching* art. You can teach people how to refine their techniques, but that's a task that would bore me. The other thing you can teach, is the history, what other artists have done. My knowledge of that subject is confined to my personal favorites. I have no real expertise. No, Joe, my philosophy is that true art has to evolve from the artist's own resources."

"Will you consider giving a guest lecture to my class at the end of the semester?"

Rather than say no, I told Joe that I'd think about it. We exchanged phone numbers over coffee and I left.

Talking with Joe had been enjoyable, but my day had otherwise turned to dust. I was still upset about being excluded from Gwen's visit and I was upset about the dismantling of the art world that I had known in Manhattan. It had happened slowly during the seven years I had been living in Northport and it shouldn't have come as such a shock, but this was the first time I had bothered to notice. I went home.

Chapter 17

Gwen had come and gone, and there was no word from Dara. There was no way of knowing if that was good or bad. I waited. My house became as desolate and unfriendly as my unused studio. Reading was out. My mind was too preoccupied with Dara's silence. I did some minor chores, but often found myself walking from room to room feeling isolated and abandoned.

By Tuesday, the wait became too oppressive, and my reluctance to contact her– because I was sulking over having been left out of the weekend plans– was no longer a match for my concern. Dara was distracted and distraught on the phone; nothing like the real Dara. She said she didn't want to talk, couldn't talk if she wanted to, because she had so much to think through before she dragged me into the fray. Then, she said something very odd. *She would call soon.* Her voice was clipped and stilted.

Nothing that Dara might have told me about Gwen's visit would have depressed me as much as that terse conversation. Dara, like Gwen, was shutting me out, too. I had already lost two of the three most important things in my life– my painting and Gwen. Now it seemed as though Dara was distancing herself from me, as well. That scared me.

In a real and frightening way, I was being successively excluded from my own life. I walked toward a canvas, the doors closed. I walked toward Gwen, the doors closed. I ran to Dara for reassurance and was cooled by the breeze of her doors shutting.

The best part of our relationship had always been the sharing. Our relationship started with talking on our walks from Dara's office to her apartment, and we had kept the conversation going for twelve years, practically non-stop. Her unwillingness to talk to me was unprecedented.

My cure for stress had always been the same. Painting!

Here I was scared, worried and depressed, so should have been in the studio producing troubled but inspired masterpieces.

I didn't paint.

I couldn't paint.

I didn't want to paint.

With no other resources at my disposal, it would have been easy to get even more depressed. Painting was always my first option, and when that hadn't worked, there had been Dara. Overreacting wasn't going to get me anywhere. I couldn't let myself fall apart over one conversation with Dara, and resolved to hold out until our next meeting with Dr. Rosenthal.

The days passed, somehow. Mo hadn't called back from wherever in the world he had gone. I called my brother Zach more times during that one week than during the past year. He suffered my assault with patience and amusement. When Dara finally called the night before our appointment, our conversation wasn't very heartwarming.

"Hi, Leo. Do you hate me?"

"No . . . not hate, worried and upset. Are you okay?"

"Relative to what? I'm not sure. It's been troubling. About tomorrow?"

"What?"

"I've got a lot to talk about with Dr. Rosenthal. Do you mind if I do all the talking?"

"Do you want me not to come?"

Dara hesitated. A little too long for me.

"No, you can come. You should hear what I have to say. It's just that you and Dr. Rosenthal were a little too chummy last time. I felt like I wasn't even a part of it."

"But he spent the last half of our session asking you questions and telling you how to deal with Gwen. I don't think I monopolized him."

"Well, I need to get this straight in my mind. I'm drained and miserable. There doesn't appear to be any way out of this for Gwen."

"I promise to listen and won't say a word."

"Okay, meet me there tomorrow." *Meet me there!*

Dara was already in Dr. Rosenthal's office when I arrived. She looked nervous and unsure, completely different from the Dara I knew. My apprehension increased.

Dara launched into her story without any preliminaries, and without saying hello to me. She spoke too quickly and the cadence was all wrong. Watching her was like watching bad theater, as if someone were reading lines without understanding them. The strangeness confused me– I felt like I was watching from a long distance, or through water, or from another dimension; something surreal. The woman sitting there was unrecognizable. There was hardly a trace of Dara in her.

She told Dr. Rosenthal that she had started according to his plan by providing a nurturing and hassle-free environment. Gwen was wary and anxious at first. She talked about T.V. and news events and nothing of herself or Marcus; nor did she answer any of Dara's casual– according to Dara– questions.

"On Saturday night, I suggested that Gwen take a bath. None of us ever lock the bathroom doors and when I knocked, Gwen invited me in. When she was a teenager, I would sometimes draw her a bath and bring her a cup of cocoa while she soaked. We had some of our most important mother/daughter conversations during those baths. I hoped to evoke the kind of childhood memory you had recommended.

"Gwen readily agreed to the idea, and I got us each a cup of cocoa, settling on the commode to chat. Gwen was neck deep in soap bubbles and, at last, looked relaxed and content.

"As she leaned forward to place her mug on the tub rim, her breasts rose out of the water for an instant. There was a large blue smudge on the left one.

"Gwen, did you bruise yourself?" Gwen slumped deeper into the suds.

"No, why?"

"I thought I saw a bruise on your breast."

"I don't have any bruises."

"Let me see."

"I told you, I DON'T HAVE ANY BRUISES! LEAVE ME ALONE!"

"Then let me see." Although she had screamed at me, I tried to remain calm.

"Go away. Leave me alone, now."

"Show me.. (I know you warned me not to push her, but she had exasperated me.)"

"No."

It was one of those arguments that go nowhere. We were both getting angrier, and angrier. Finally, Gwen rose out of the tub and said, "Well, look then."

As the bubbles gradually rolled off her breast, exposing the bare skin, Dara could see an amateur tattoo of *Marcus* across the upper part of Gwen's left breast.

Dara lost it.

Gwen stood there dripping water and soap, majestic in her scorn. Dara had to turn away in disgust and horror. Despite Dr. Rosenthal's counseling, and knowing that she was doing the wrong thing, she couldn't stop herself. She took the one-way jump into maternal oblivion.

"Did he do this to you?"

"I asked him to. Anyway, it's none of your business."

"Does Marcus have your name tattooed on him?"

"I love belonging to Marcus. You wouldn't understand. You've never understood me. You were always so wrapped up with Leo that you never took the time to understand me."

"Belong?" That was the only part that registered with Dara. Later, she remembered the whole thing.

Gwen grabbed a towel and pushed past Dara. She slammed the door to her room. Fifteen minutes later, she emerged with her overnight bag.

"Where are you going?"

"Home. I've called a cab."

"But it's too late. There are no more trains tonight."

"They're going to let me stay at the motel. I'm clearly not welcome here."

"Nonsense, you'll always be . . . "

"No, Mom. Your version of Gwen is welcome. That's not who I am anymore. I'm all grown up now, and have a family of my own. You don't approve of my family, of Marcus. Tough. I'm out of here."

"Gwen, don't go. Not like this. Let's talk. Please?"

"There's nothing to talk about. Marcus is right. He always is. You just want to control me. I hear my cab. I'm going."

"What about your phone number? Can I have it?"

"It won't do you any good. We're moving."

She ran out the door.

When Dara finished her account, the office rang with an ominous silence. Dr. Rosenthal sat at his desk with his eyes closed, tapping a pencil eraser against the blotter. Dara looked like she was about to collapse. Someone needed to say something to dispel the negative energy in the room, but I knew better than to break my promise to Dara. Instead, I crossed over to stand behind her and rested my hand on her shoulder. Dara pushed my hand away and said, in an annoyed tone, "Not now, Leo." I skulked back to my chair. Dr. Rosenthal looked at me quizzically. I just stared back.

"Not exactly as we had planned it, eh Dara? The important thing is that you tried your best. And from what you've told me, most of it went well. Don't beat yourself over this. It's never easy to break the mythos of a controlling and dominant figure. It would have been nice if Gwen had been reading from the same script as we were, but it looks like she's locked into Marcus's script for now. We just need to regroup and try a new tactic."

"It's hopeless."

"Gwen's alive and young and resilient. That rules out *hopeless*. Are there any other friends or relatives to whom Gwen is close, who could help?"

Dara looked sheepish. "There's only me . . . (pause, pause), and, I suppose, Leo." My reaction to the *I suppose* didn't go unnoticed by Dr. Rosenthal.

The good doctor suggested that Dara concentrate on coming to terms with her own emotions and self-recrimination before tackling the difficult task of helping Gwen. He gave her some writing assignments and another appointment. When we got up to leave, he called me back.

"Dara, wait for me for a minute. I'll be right there."

"Dara will be meeting alone with me from now on, Leo. If that makes you feel left out, in fact, you are. It's merely the situation and not the people involved. Gwen and Dara aren't rejecting *you*, so don't take it personally. Right now, the two of them have to deal with the problem between them. If you're having problems dealing with your role in all this, I'd be happy to recommend another psychiatrist for you." I had just been summarily dismissed.

"Just one more thing. Do you think it's a good idea to take Dara away for a while to distract her, even if the distraction is only temporary?"

"You know Dara better than I do, Leo. What do you think she'd like? Go with your instincts."

Our conversation lasted less than three minutes, but when I went out to the reception area, Dara was gone.

Chapter 18

Things didn't get any better over the next few weeks. Dara didn't know where Gwen was, and she continued to blame herself, uncharacteristically wallowing in her despair.

My daily calls were dismissed. Dara wouldn't talk to me because it was a 'bad time' for her. Gwen's problem was now secondary for me to our problem. Gwen's situation didn't appear to have a solution, so my energy was devoted to salvaging our relationship.

If Dara had found someone else and had left me for him, my misery would have been equal, but I would have done nothing. You can tell someone that they can't stop loving you or that they are obligated to still love you.

That's not what this was. Dara had shut me off and out because she couldn't separate her feelings about Gwen from all her other relationships.

Perhaps it was pure ego, but I really believed that my company would have been the best thing for Dara. Being unable to help Dara frustrated me more than my own simple frustration over not being with her. I called Dr. Rosenthal for advice. He wouldn't say much because of *patient confidentiality issues.* Dr. Rosenthal was one more person to close the door on me. He sympathized with me *for the way I must be feeling*, and advised for me to be there, if I could hold on, for when Dara did want my support.

I was the abused party in all this– the all-giving altruist to Dara's selfish, self-indulgent ingrate– and it was starting to get to me. All I wanted to do was love and support Dara, and she wouldn't even talk to me. Angry, but deep down I didn't want to be mad, so suppressed my anger. Or is it mad-ness? Or madness?

Pretending that Dara's reaction to Gwen's plight had not affected her feelings toward me, I scheduled an SST flight to Paris and two weeks at the George V hotel. In all the years we were together, we'd never been away for any length of time, mainly because I had never been able to go without painting, but also because Dara was as unwilling to leave her own work for more than a day or two. Twenty-something years after I had lived in Paris for two years, the time had come to actually see the city.

Since Dara wasn't talking to me by phone, my only recourse was to invite her to Paris with me, in person. She wasn't there on Saturday morning when I arrived. Letting myself in with my own key seemed inappropriate under the circumstances so I grabbed a patio chair from out back and brought it to the front lawn to wait. Besides, I didn't want to see something inside that would devastate me– like another man's clothes or naked body, or slashed up shreds of *Junction*.

Dara showed up twenty minutes later, in running clothes and out of breath. She approached from behind me so I didn't see her until she half caressed, half brushed the back of my head as she passed. She had already passed by, and had her back to me as I stood up to greet her.

I followed her inside. She didn't look particularly surprised to see me.

"Dara, I --."

"Shower, first," she cut me off, and disappeared inside. That was a warm greeting!

"Want some company?" What I meant was, *come on Dara, it's me.*

"Have some coffee. I'll be back in a few minutes." (*Fuck off, bozo!*)

There had to be someone else. I grabbed a cup of coffee as a prop in case I got caught snooping, and looked around for the telltale signs of Dara's new boyfriend. The replacement lover was either a fastidious neatness freak, or else nonexistent– the angel on my right shoulder campaigned for the latter, the devil on my left shoulder didn't have to say a word.

Dara returned, looking thin and tired. Her eyes were the scariest part. In their glory, Dara's eyes sparkled and probed, and bespoke of intelligence, self-assurance and ease. Even at their worst, they were haunting and bottomless. But today, Dara's eyes were shallow and unsure. They darted where once they danced. They'd been on fire, now they looked consumed. The pallette of her portrait shifted to the somber hues.

"Nice to see you, Leo." The way you'd say it to the IRS agent at the audit.

"I can't do small talk with you, Dara. Can't we talk for real? Like Dara and Leo?"

"I'm too confused to make sense to myself, how can I make sense to anyone else?"

"I don't think of myself as *anyone else* when it comes to you."

"This isn't about you, Leo, not this time. I can't be with you when I feel this way about myself."

"Why not? I don't understand. Two weeks ago, there was no clear distinction between you and me. There were two bodies and one us. And it worked for us because there was never any separation between what bothered Dara and what bothered Leo, what was good for Dara and what was good for Leo. I know you're suffering now, but believe me, all I want to do is to make you happy, and do whatever I can to make you feel better. Share this with me. We both need that."

"Not this time, Leo. You weren't the overconfident mother who did this to her child. You weren't the arrogant headstrong woman who couldn't even imagine a defect in herself."

"So you're telling me that you're willing to sacrifice us to Gwen? And do you think sacrificing me will change what happens to Gwen? You're feeling so sorry for yourself and so depressed that you're doing the exact opposite of what is good for you. Right now, you're not helping yourself *or* Gwen. At least let me be there so you have one friend in your camp."

"I've got a therapist, Leo, I don't need another one; especially not an amateur. I haven't stopped loving you, so you can get off of your *why me* soapbox. It's just that I can't devote any of my energy to anyone– yes, even you, right now. If we have as good a relationship as you say, it will survive this. For now, though, it has to be on hold."

"I didn't come here to fight, but to give you this. Though I'm not your therapist, I think it would be good for you to get away from here and, yes, to be with me for a while. We've never been away together, and I'm hoping to, at last, be able to answer all your questions about Paris." I offered her the plane ticket, the usual red, white and blue folder to which I had– and which now seemed unfortunate that I had– added a stick-on bright green bow.

"I told you that I can't do something like that right now. I'm too upset."

"So you think it's better to stay here and wallow in your sadness? Well, it's not doing Gwen any good, and it's not doing you any good. Even an amateur can see that you've gotten worse since you've been in therapy. You dismiss my ability to help you, but won't give me the chance to try." The great leap from sheer altruism to uncompromising anger turned out to be a smaller jump than I thought.

"I'd love to go to Paris with you someday. But not now."

"Maybe another twelve years like the sex thing." I had been divorced for more than twenty years, but the crushing parries that Sylvie had taught me to deliver rose to the surface with no coaxing. I was more angry with Dara than I had ever been in my life; I wasn't, however, proud of myself for reflexively sinking to meanness. Dara just looked at me with tears welling up in her eyes.

"Look, Dara, that was stupid, I'm not your enemy, I'm your friend– your best friend. I'm going on this trip anyway. You can decide to come with me up to the last minute; you can even join me there. I'll be at the Georges Cinq." I threw her ticket down on the table and left.

Two weeks later I was jetting my way to Paris. Alone– my supersonic flight left even sound behind us– and with no word from Dara. Determined to have a good time, to do for myself what this trip was supposed to do for Dara– get away from all the old shit and just have a good time.

The first day didn't bode well because all my energy was spent looking over my shoulder to see if Dara was coming. But the trip was designed as a totally indulgent luxury vacation for two, and it was easy to allow myself to slip into the aura of Paris and the niceties of my surroundings. Before long, I was having a great time.

Paris is a wonderful city filled with excitement and well-dressed people. The downside was how romantic it is, so had to stop myself when my thought drifted, all too often, to Dara.

During my two years in Paris, I had managed to miss just about everything except the University and my old dorm. The dorm was gone and no one at the University knew who I was other than by my reputation. They were cordial, but mostly disinterested. I didn't dawdle there.

Besides two day trips, to Versailles and the Loire Valley, I flew to Prague to meet up with Mo and Barbara who had been on one extended trip since leaving New York. They were in a let's-not-travel-like-fat-cat-tourists mode, and were staying at a much less elegant hotel than the Georges V. Still, it had a very European feel to it, and my room was comfortable and large.

We toured Prague together for three days. Barbara demonstrated an easy and witty storytelling ability, and our conversations alternated between stories of their travels and the Dara-Gwen-Leo saga.

"We usually begin discussions about couples by asking *whom do we know, besides Dara and Leo, who have a good marriage?*"

Mo saw the tightening of my jaw.

"That little bastard not only screwed up Gwen's life, but he's come between you and Dara. He's an evil son-of-a-bitch, isn't he?"

"I don't know, Mo. He hasn't really done anything wrong from his perspective, or broken any laws. As for Dara and me, he can't have planned for that."

"I don't know either, but if someone was bent on completely destroying a family, he couldn't do much better. Except for death or financial ruin, and I hope you've taken care of your money."

"This trip is supposed to keep me from thinking about all that. Tell me more about Venice."

Leaving Prague was difficult. The city was interesting and beautiful with nice people, and I'd forgotten how much I loved just talking with people who cared about me. Mo and Barbara were anxious to get back to Utah to see their new granddaughter, so couldn't be talked into returning with me to Paris, or staying for a few more days in Prague. I returned to Paris alone.

Chapter 19

The rest of my stay was more of the same. I spent so much time at the Louvre and the Musee d'Orsay, that the guards not only stopped eyeing me suspiciously, but began greeting me. My fascination with my long-postponed exploration of Paris made me understand why people liked to travel so much, and I embarked on the trip home feeling good about myself and the world.

A curious thing, curious *and* momentous, happened on the flight back. While nursing a drink and having sort of a conversation with my seat mate– he was working at a laptop computer, but occasionally paused to share a few words with me–. I was distractedly sketching on a napkin, not really aware of what I was drawing.

A steward stopped by to check on my brandy.

"Wow, that's a great drawing. Look at those eyes. Is she real or a fantasy?"

Looking down at my napkin, there was Dara staring back at me, the way she looked on the day we met. Her face on my napkin startled me because I wasn't aware that I had been thinking about her. Whom was I kidding? She had been on my mind almost constantly– if not consciously, then certainly in the juicy marshes of my subconscious.

"I'll know when I get home."

A normal man would have pondered the sketch, become nostalgic for the good times with the woman pictured so vividly on the page, or fallen, swoonlike, into a dark depression for what was no more. Leo Schultz is far from a normal man, he is a painter. I wanted, no needed to paint those eyes. That startled me again. *Paint* those eyes. The smell of the oils filled my nostrils, the creamy canvas turned into those eyes behind my own closed lids. I wanted to paint!

Paint.

Me. I wanted to paint. Exuberant and innervated, I halfway stood, as if ready to run back to my studio. The steward regretted his casual remark that had triggered my effusive reaction. He began to apologize.

"No, no. Don't apologize. I'm very happy. It's hard to explain, but I seem to be on track again."

Because I was going home to paint.

To paint Dara!

A canvas stood ready on my easel within seconds of getting out of the limousine. No matter that I was still travel worn and disheveled from my flight. Anyone else would have showered and changed. Rested or relaxed. Leo painted.

And painted.

And painted.

Painted until the canvas was covered with Dara. Dara and Dara's eyes. She came to me via paint because she wasn't available any other way. I painted in a trance, nonstop for almost three days until it was done. When it was complete, I didn't even stop to look at the canvas. I didn't need to. I had lived with it for three days. No, I had lived with it for fifteen years.

Putting the wet canvas aside, I immediately reached for another. There were more Daras in me, many more Daras. With a few broad strokes Dara was standing in front of *Jasmine* with a glass of champagne in her hand at my opening party. Finally exhausted, I had to stop to sleep.

The next morning found me both exhilarated and depressed— exhilarated because I was painting again, depressed because I missed Dara so much. My head was so crowded with different images of Dara that I wrote them down so I wouldn't try to paint them all at once.

When I stopped to think— only after a great deal more feverish painting— I realized that Dara might not approve. Two months ago, it wouldn't have been an issue. Now, I didn't know.

Facing her rejection one more time, and though her consent was immaterial— there was no way I could stop— the request for permission was an excuse to call her. Dara was as reluctant to talk to me as she had been before my trip to France.

"Wait, Dara, don't hang up. One question. This is important."

"What is it?" I asked myself, *Why, exactly, do I want to paint this awful woman?*

"I, uh, I'm painting again."

"You are? That's great. I'm happy for you."

"You."

"What?"

"I'm painting . . . that is, I want to paint you."

"Why?"

"I can't believe you're asking me that. If you have to ask, there is no answer. Or, because like all my paintings, I have to. Anyway, is it all right with you?"

"I can't sit for you right now."

"I don't need you to sit. Just your permission."

"Nudity?"

"Maybe. I won't show a single painting to anyone until you've seen them. Any painting you don't like, you can destroy."

"You know I'd never destroy anything you painted."

"Then I'll destroy them. Or bury them somewhere, or whatever. Do I have your permission?"

"No one tells Leo Shultz what to paint or not paint; not Dara Harrington, not Mo, not any sane person. We'll talk about the paintings later. I've got to go."

Not exactly the warm reception I wanted, something more like, *why don't I come over so you can refresh your memory about my thighs?* Still, she had given me her permission to paint. She was right, though. If she'd said *no*, that wouldn't have stopped me.

So began the largest series of paintings of my career.

My obsessive painting of Dara was more than a little sick. It was voyeuristic and perverse. The real Dara, whom I both longed for and hated because she had abandoned me was unobtainable. So I created her with oils, choosing her expression, choosing her positioning, forcing her to be with me. Those paintings were torture to paint, but I couldn't stop.

I painted.

Painting wasn't enough to fill the void left by Dara's self-imposed exile. The physical act of painting exhausted me. so I couldn't paint continuously. And yet, I had no down time; that is, no down time of value. I wasn't talking to people, or going out, and I wasn't feeling good. Painting and moping were all I did.. Mostly I painted.

Joe Bernington at the New School still wanted me to talk to his class. Joe was enthusiastic when I called, and suggested a small talk on any subject that interested me followed by questions, and, if

I didn't mind, critiquing the students' paintings. Helping Joe would break the cycle of the rut of my despair.

The students maintained their interest during my talk about evoking a message with paint, as opposed to evoking it with symbolism, and the difference between symbolism in art and art as symbolism.

The question period was less enlightening. Most questions were directed toward how they could become successful (") as artists, assuming they could gain money and fame– always in that order, like you know who– if they had the magic words I knew. I couldn't offer much help there.

Commenting on their work was tricky because I am not an art critic or a trained instructor, and I judge art on a personal level– what grabs my interest and makes me want to come back and look again. Restricting my comments to only the paintings that appealed to me; I explained that I wasn't saying the others weren't Great Art, merely that they didn't captivate me.

Many of the students were very talented and two of them stood out in particular. One was a woman who painted still-lifes with such an amazing use of color that the paintings crossed all boundaries and were at once still-life, abstractions and surreal. The other artist was a more classical surrealist. His paintings were so layered that you could look at them a hundred times and see something new each time. They weren't crowded with symbolism, they were quite literal in a way, and yet they weren't. I was impressed and intrigued.

My comments centered on those two artists, with limited references to a few others as well. A very young, very tall, very dark, very attractive woman approached me when I was done.

"You didn't mention my work. Did they frighten you?" She had brought in almost a dozen medium sized canvasses that were close-up views of penises and vaginas. The penises were all adorned with artifacts such as cock-rings, or ribbons, or sprigs of flowers. The vaginas all had something different inserted in them. The work was technically okay. The skin did appear to be alive, and the perspective, though stark, was accurate..

"Your work is a political statement. To me, it's not art."

"Art can't be political?"

"Not if that's all it is. If it's political because it's breaking into a new frontier of art like the cubists did, that's still art. If it's political like *Guernica* and still great art, I like that too. I find your work too gimmicky. You're saying, *look at what I can paint. I'm liberated. I'm not afraid to paint this!*"

"So, obviously, you're afraid of sex?"

"I don't look at sex as something to fear or not fear. What fun would it be to have sex with someone who had to conquer her fears to have sex with me. Fear should never enter into a sexual situation, which is not to say that I wouldn't practice safe sex. Does that make me afraid?"

"You're equivocating. Do you want to fuck me?"

"There you go again. You're being your paintings. In my face. The shock value. I don't know the answer to your question. I don't know you at all. Unlike you, I'm not just about penises and vaginas. I'm a whole package kind of guy."

"You're showing your age."

"I am my age, why pretend otherwise?"

"How about this, then? There's an opening tonight at the Ritch Gallery in Soho. Come with me and get to know me. Then I'll ask you again."

"What if I still say no?"

"Your loss. I'll find someone else."

Carrie, my "date," took me to the gallery. In the past, everyone there would have been familiar, but that night I only recognized one or two of the uptown gallery owners. The others were a sea of anonymous faces. Except.

Carrie had nothing to say that interested me. The opening had very little to do with the displayed photographs– most of the people were there to be seen and weren't even making a pretense of looking at the photographs– which weren't very good. With little to see, and bored by Carrie's company, my attention was distracted by a woman across the room who had her back to me. The way she moved brought up images from my past. I was almost certain that I was looking at Ellen.

I kept waiting for the woman to turn, but she never did. As I continued to watch her, there was no doubt. Carrie noticed my distraction and looked annoyed. Undeterred by her glare, I excused myself and walked over to my old girlfriend.

My heart beat rapidly. In order to see her face, I had to insinuate myself between Ellen and the others. As soon as I confirmed her Ellen-ness, she saw me.

"Leo!" She turned toward me and we kissed.

A passionate kiss.

Chapter 20

"Ellen, it's good to see you. Are you talking to me?"

"Where were you when I just kissed you? It's been over twelve years. I've let go. How have you been?"

"Mostly good. I wouldn't have expected to see you here. You look great."

"There aren't a lot of places where a single woman can go alone. I take advantage of everything."

"So, you're not with anyone?"

"No, I realized long ago that I was going to be alone. I never really fit with anyone, even you, although I did think so for a while. No one has ever lasted more than a few months."

"Are you happy?"

"As much as anyone."

Carrie was malevolently eyeing Ellen and me, while I tried to ignore her. Finally she strode over to us, and placed her hand on my hip.

"I'm going home, to bed. Are you coming with me?"

"Thanks for the invitation, but no."

She shrugged as she gave Ellen the once over– Ellen, who was still a beautiful woman even though she must have been twenty-five years older than Carrie– with a body every bit as hard and toned as it ever was.

"Well, you're going to miss the best fuck of your life." Ellen and I both laughed out loud. Carrie shrugged again and walked away from us. She was on a mission, trolling for fairer game. Ellen looked at me.

"Actually, you were the best *I* ever had."

"Ellen, we should talk. Do you want to go someplace?"

"How about my place?" Her previous comment, and the kiss we'd shared, made me wary.

"To talk?"

"To talk."

On the way to Ellen's, she told me she was approaching twenty-five years at the watch company and would be eligible for retirement, but she wasn't ready.

She had become very friendly with her brother who was recently widowed after more than forty years of marriage. Ellen and her brother had never been close because he was quite a bit older. Now they shared the same circle of friends and socialized together, often.

Not until we had settled down with a glass of wine in her living room, did she ask me to fill her in on my life.

"Got a few hours? It's been a bad year."

"I've got as long as you need. Are you still with Dara?"

"I wish I knew."

"Now you've hooked me. Tell me everything."

I did. All about Gwen and Marcus and Dara and me, and my inability to paint, and my trip to France. Ellen stopped me from time to time to ask a pointed question or to clarify a detail. By the time I had finished, we'd gone through two bottles of wine and most of a bottle of vodka. It was past three in the morning, and I was exhausted, but more from the emotional stress of recounting everything than from the actual talking and the late hour. The heavy drinking only made things worse. I asked Ellen if I could crash at her place for the night. She smiled slyly.

"You can if you sleep with me."

"Ellen, I just finished telling you about me and Dara. Though it may be over, I'm not over her. I doubt that I'll ever be."

"I heard everything you said. Just come to bed with me. No strings. Let's just see what happens. It's late, maybe we'll both fall asleep."

We didn't. We danced our old dance.

I awoke the next morning both hung over and anxious, realizing that having sex with Ellen had been very irresponsible– irresponsible to Ellen, myself and Dara. To add to my discomfort, Ellen began to stir and nuzzled close to me in a too familiar way.

We snuggled in that not unenjoyable manner until Ellen was fully awake. I disengaged from her and turned to face her.

"That was stupid of me. I'm a cad and a rake. I can only apologize." Ellen put her outstretched fingers on my lower abdomen as she answered.

"This may not be an ideal situation for me, Leo, but, first of all, it was my idea, and I don't regret that. I wasn't kidding when I said that the best sex of my life was with you– certainly, no one since has been as good. Nothing would please me more than if you realized how truly terrific I am and dumped Dara, or at least get her out of your mind. I was honest about needing to be alone, and not live with or marry anyone. Still, it would be nice to keep you as a friend."

"I like being your friend, Ellen. But you got hurt once and I'm reluctant to put you in a situation where it may happen again. I'm surprised that you've forgiven me for the last time."

"Only on some levels. It would have been easier if you'd become a monk after me. But, no, you left me for Love. I'd still try to lure you away from Dara if I thought it would do any good."

"I don't know what to say."

"That's all right. I didn't expect a reply. Here's a deal for you, though."

"What kind of deal?"

"A trade. I give you something and you give me something."

"Like?"

"My boss plays golf with Mark Cleamons, the CEO of Marcus' company. I'll introduce you. Why don't you see if he'll help you locate Marcus and Gwen?"

"Good idea. And what do I give you?"

Her hand moved downward.

Chapter 21

Dara was mired in regret, blaming herself for everything that had happened to Gwen, sinking lower and lower to the point of losing her quintessential Dara-ness. She'd always been the person you would want on hand during a crisis. Now, she was the crisis. Dara had always been sane, solid, resolute and quick to find a solution because she always believed there was one. Evidently, when it came to Gwen, none of that held true– she'd become increasingly dysfunctional since Gwen got married.

Though deep down I felt that Marcus was pure evil and had some malevolent goal, there was a small part of me that wondered whether all his presumed evil was not just the way he was reacting to Dara, and maybe me, too. Perhaps Marcus was merely trying to distance his new bride, and himself, from her overbearing mother. Maybe what we viewed as evil was just a brutally blunt rejection of Dara's dominance in Gwen's life.

My continued phone calls were dutifully recorded on her answer machine and never returned. The receptionist at her office told me that Dara was on *an indefinite leave of absence.* The woman was startled to learn that I didn't know. There would be fresh gossip that day.

Gwen had caused all the major changes in Dara's life. Events in Gwen's life had been responsible for all the significant upheavals in Dara's. Dara's pregnancy had sealed Dara's estrangement from her family. Gwen's birth caused Dara to give up drugs and a wild life to become a highly successful graphic artist. She was the reason why Dara did such an about face on her sexuality and became sexually phobic. She wanted to bring up her daughter to be completely different from the way she had been. Gwen's elopement was what finally made Dara regain her sexual being. And the stress of Gwen's chosen lifestyle is what had caused the rift between us.

My obsession with my paintings of her– in a way that I had never been obsessed before– should have been a huge warning sign. The repeated visions of Dara had become too important to me. I hadn't been only half of the Dara-Leo continuum in almost fifteen years, and I wasn't handling the separation very well. The paintings conjured up Dara in my lonely life; I would have cuddled with them if I could. They were no longer just art, they had a being of their own, which I related to on a subconscious psychosexual level. I even talked to them; talking to Dara by proxy, by way of an oil paint hyperspace.

There were twenty-eight paintings in all, arranged all around my studio, completely eclipsing *Jasmine.* Only two were nudes, and a third one that was in a category all by itself. Dara was about her eyes, not about her skin.

The first nude depicted the first time I'd seen Dara completely naked, done in a dream-like, backlit impressionistic style with soft colors and fluid, and almost indistinct borders. Anyone could tell that the painter was in love with his subject– verging, at least to me, on pathetic because it conveyed such longing.

The second was a painting of Dara chest deep in a bath– no bubbles, just translucent water– that could have represented any period in her life when, after a long and stressful day, she relaxed in the tub. You could feel the heat of the water melt the stress off her face and see that stress slowly being replaced with calm and relaxation.

The third nude is not really part of the series because it was meant only for me. I intended to burn it on my death bed. The painting was great, but the sickest I had done, not because of its content, but for the masturbatory and self-flagellant feelings of the artist (not generally described in full in the show catalog). The canvas depicted Dara's sexual epiphany the night I awoke to find her astride me– erotic and terrifying, sensual and foreboding. Dara looked magnificent. The perspective was my perspective as I had looked up at her. The painting took its place, for now, among the others, but every time I looked at it, every time I even caught a glimpse of it in the corner of my vision, I sobbed uncontrollably.

To save my sanity –the excuse I told myself– I saw Ellen on a regular, if infrequent, basis. Ellen was always pleased when I called, but the sex was more like two actors playing the role of ballerinas rather than the ballerinas actually dancing, themselves. Still, it was worthy of an Oscar.

Michael Cleamons, Ellen's contact, was very sympathetic to my story, and offered to bring Marcus to the home office and arrange for me to meet him. He regretted that Marcus was presently involved in some plans that had close deadlines, but would get him to New York in about a month. Marcus' record only had his address and phone number in Oregon– no information about his family life.

In the meantime, I continued to indulge my two manias that had, by circumstance and inevitability, become one.

I painted Dara.

Michael Cleamons greeted me warmly on the morning of the day that I finally met Marcus. He ordered coffee for us as we sat together in a board room.

"I've known Richard for years. He's spoken about you many times."

I had no idea whom he meant, at first. No one, not even Barbara, ever calls Mo anything but *Mo*; not if the person knows him at all.

"Are you friends?"

"No, but we've had some business dealings from time to time."

I'd have to ask Mo why he'd never thought about Cleamons when we were first trying to find out about Marcus.

"This problem with Mr. Davis upsets me. I don't like my people to present a bad image to the public on either a business or personal level."

"As far as I know, he hasn't done anything illegal, and he, maybe with good reason, probably feels that he hasn't done anything dishonest or immoral. His actions perplex me, though. Why has he avoided meeting either his wife's mother or me? I want to get to the bottom of that. The last thing I want is for Marcus to lose his job, which would affect our daughter and their new baby, too."

"Well, let's see what he has to say for himself. He's already in the building and has been directed up here."

As Marcus came through the door, his face slipped through a spectrum of expressions. First, he showed concern (being called to see the CEO), alarm when he recognized me, then annoyance. The transformations took place in only a few seconds before he became Mr. Congeniality.

Michael Cleamons went through the unnecessary introductions before excusing himself.

"Stop by my office on your way out, Marcus. My secretary has some things she needs to go over with you. Nice to meet you, Mr. Schultz." We shook.

The *stop by my office* thing was a nice precaution. It prevented Marcus from bolting as soon as his boss left.

Marcus was as nice as can be. He smiled warmly as he leaned across the conference table to shake my hand.

"Leo, so good to meet you, at last. It's been a long time coming. How ya doin'?"

"We haven't met because you refused to meet me. You even convinced Gwen to exclude me from her life."

"Nonsense, Leo. The time was never quite right. What with my demanding job and all the travel, and Gwen's pregnancy, and being newly wed and then moving. I've been spread so thin. Sorry if I've upset you."

"How is Gwen? Has the baby come yet? Is Gwen happy?"

"Well, I'll tell you, Leo. Gwen's got one of those postpartum depression things, but the baby is beautiful. We call her Carole Dara after our mothers. Won't Dara like that? "

"She'd much prefer to see the baby. And Gwen."

"Of course, of course. That will come. I've just got to get Gwennie through this depression thing. But I think I've got the handle on it. Gwen just needs structure. I'm afraid I let up too much when Carrie was born. My little love machine needs a lot of direction, you know? For a start, she's pregnant again. That'll get her on the right track."

"Pregnant? Again? How old is Car . . . er . . . Carrie?"

"Three months. Why?"

"Don't you think it's a little too soon, a little overwhelming? Especially with Gwen feeling depressed?"

"No, not at all. It's just the thing she needs. Besides, I want bunches of children, and Gwen knows I get grumpy when I don't get my way. She knows what she has to do."

Marcus smiled that maddening smile all the while he was spouting that garbage– a smile I wanted to wipe off his face with a machete. That was precisely the reaction he was after, so I played the game too. Marcus invited me to lunch.

He took me to an unmarked restaurant on the ninth floor of a nondescript building off of Wall Street. An insider's place. As we were escorted to our table, Marcus waved to tables we passed, and said hello to several patrons. No one responded as if they knew him, making me suspect that he was putting on a show for my benefit. Marcus was dressed in a very expensive looking pinstriped suit, probably Armani, and a beautiful silk tie. His shoes were highly polished, his bright white shirt was creaseless. From what I knew about his job, I couldn't imagine where he was getting that kind of money. His real job required clothes more like boots and a hard hat.

We ordered lunch. Marcus declined a drink because he had *lots of clients to contact this afternoon.* I declined because I wanted to remember every detail to report back to Dara (you remember Dara, don't you, Leo?). For the most part, Marcus maintained his maddening grin. From time to time, it slipped and didn't quite hide the Helter Skelter look in his eyes. I asked him about his family.

"I'm not very close with my parents because I never respected my father. He was very lax with my mother. She'd been married before, and he never made her answer for that. Mom did whatever she wanted, and Dad never acted like a man." It was my first glimpse of Manson. "A man would have taken control."

"Do you like your mother?"

"As a kid, but then she turned on me. When I was a teenager, I tried to provide what my wimpy father had failed to do. Like all women, my mother needed structure and discipline. She had been so spoiled that she reacted badly to my attempts at undoing the damage, and my gutless father was too weak to back me up." That Manson look again.

I thought it prudent to change the subject, but there weren't too many safe directions to go.

"So, Marcus. When I tell Dara that I had a chance to meet you, she's going to want to visit Gwen and the baby. Is that going to be a problem?"

"No, not at all. As long as she understands the rules."

"Which are?"

"Okay. One: She only comes for one or two days. Two: She stays in a hotel. Our trailer (trailer!) is too small for more than us. Three: She comes alone. I won't have my child exposed to fornication and illicit relationships. Four: She doesn't fill Gwen's head with feminist crap. It just confuses Gwennie, then I have to discipline her more."

My untouched lunch underscored my growing nausea. I ordered a drink, after all. Marcus' garbage was unforgettable, and I needed to quell my mounting anger. Lunch continued with the same flavor– mostly that of bile– until, finally and mercifully, it was time to go. Marcus paid the bill and shook my hand.

"It was a pleasure to talk with you, Leo. Can I call you when I'm back in New York?"

"Sure. When do you think that will be?" Despite my revulsion, I wanted to keep the line of communication open.

"I don't know, I'm planning a little vacation. Work has been hectic lately."

"That may be just what Gwen needs, too. You know, if you two want to go away alone, I bet Dara would come to Oregon to take care of Carrie."

"Gwen's not going, just me. She hasn't earned a vacation yet."

"I see."

I didn't see.

Chapter 22

Dara didn't respond to my call to tell her about my lunch with Marcus. Knowing she would call back if I left a message about what I had learned, I only left my name, still hoping she would want to talk to me because she wanted to, and not just to get information about Gwen.

Keeping my news from Dara was unfair and childish. Assuming that we would get together again, why commit a crime that might haunt our relationship to eternity?

My next message was more direct. "Please call. I've met Marcus."

She called.

"What was he like? What did he say? How's Gwen? What about the baby?" So this is what is meant by *blurting*.

"Gwen has a three-month-old daughter named Carole Dara."

"We have to talk. I need to hear everything."

"I can come right over." My haughty stance ceded to my need for Dara

"No, not here. Why don't we meet at the Ferris Wheel for lunch?"

"Why won't you let me come over? I promise not to beat, badger or rape you. What are you afraid of?"

"Not now, Leo. I can't be with you right now, just give me the information."

"In which case, here it is, and the next time you'll ever hear from me is when you call me. And, while I have your ear, at last, there's a few more things I'm going to say. You desperately need help. I don't know if you're still seeing Dr. Rosenthal, but if you are, he's not the right therapist for you. You've gotten much worse. You need a psychiatrist who can prescribe medicine, antidepressants, to get you under control so you'll be able to heal yourself. Do us both a favor, and get some appropriate help."

"If you were anyone else, I would have hung up on you."

"You would have hung up on me in an instant if I didn't have information you want." I told her all I knew and all I had intuited.

"Thanks, Leo."

"Good-bye, Dara."

"No . . . I don't want . . . Leo?"

"That's completely up to you, now." I hung up.

My bluff made me feel sick. Jumping off the tightrope with no idea whether there would be a net wasn't my forte— not with Dara, not with us. I couldn't move from the phone and could scarcely breathe. The paralysis gave way to uncontrolled sobbing. My tears were about everything. Everything that had happened to Dara and to me and to Gwen. Three lives that might have been ruined by a psychotic jerk. A nobody. A nothing. And yet, he had done all this. Was it just the effects of sheer evil on things it touched, or was there a plan? And if there was, what was it?

Our lives hadn't been perfect. We had worried about Gwen, and had our little annoyances and scares– the fugues, Dara's biopsy–

but, all in all, we had a wonderful life. We were both doing what we loved professionally, we were healthy and we had all the money we could use. Most important, we had each other. If someone had set out to undo that, to destroy the three of us, he couldn't have done a better job than Marcus.

I thought about Marcus' behavior a lot, but couldn't get an angle on it. Instead, I continued to itemize my subconscious for posterity.

I painted.

In the past few weeks, Ellen had been coming out to Northport for an occasional weekend, starting when she called one day to ask if we could get together.

"I'd love to, Ellen, but I'm almost finished with a painting, and you know how crazy I get at this point. I can't relax until it's done."

"Then, uh, how about if I come out there? I'll understand if you don't want me to."

"It's not that I don't want to see you. It's just not such a good idea. You know what I'm painting. How will it make you feel to have Dara literally in your face all weekend? I know I wouldn't feel comfortable."

"Oh, her again. Yeah. That would be weird." Silence for a few seconds.

"How about this? I don't go anywhere near your studio. I don't interfere with your painting. And when you're not painting, we spend time together?"

"What will you do while I'm painting?"

"I don't know. Read in the sun, drive around, burn Dara's house down. I'll find something."

Talk about weird. I painted all day while Ellen read and suntanned naked on the deck. When I took a break, I left Dara on the easel and had sex with Ellen on the chaise. Then it was back to Dara, too insane to realize the perversity. I don't know *what* Ellen was thinking, but this must have been part of some grander plan if she was willing to subject herself to the moral abuse.

"God, Leo, does everyone have a plan against you? Marcus? Ellen? Okay, so you can add paranoia to the list of the causes of your rapid demise." I asked myself.

Although we didn't communicate on a soul to soul level, like you know who, we communicated perfectly on a social and physical level. By *social,* I mean that we could talk for hours about anything. She was smart and well informed and witty– just fun to be around. By *physical*, I mean physical.

In my few lucid moments, I knew my treatment of Ellen was headed toward hurting her again as when we broke up years before, but that didn't stop me. Ellen provided the emotional stroking– and, yes, the physical stroking– for which I was desperate. In my defense, she claimed to know what she was doing and where she was going, and was willing to accept the consequences. Though she was setting herself up, I convinced myself that I believed her.

For the next couple of months, my life consisted of Dara on the easel, Ellen on the deck and Marcus at lunch. Marcus had taken to calling me every few weeks to invite me for lunch. I always accepted in order to hear news about Gwen. In fact, Marcus was a more constant companion than Ellen.

Lunch with Marcus was always the same. For starters, we always went to the same restaurant, probably because he somehow got the company to pay for it. Marcus continued to display his sycophantic grin while spouting male chauvinist dogma that was obsolete decades before, but which never failed to bring that depraved look to his eyes. He always came with an agenda, as though he determined, beforehand, just how much and what kind of information he wanted to impart during lunch And he always presented it in a way that would elicit the most shock value.

For instance, Marcus told me that he had left Gwen– in the trailer, six months pregnant, with an infant and with no income– and was living with (off?) a girlfriend to *teach Gwen a lesson* and, get this, *get her out of her depression,* which was *getting on my nerves.*

"How do you expect her to manage?"

"She's got you to help."

"You told her that you wanted me out of her life."

"It's up to you. You can help her, or let her fend for herself. It's all the same to me."

"You also told me that you love Gwen."

"I do. But she's got to learn how to behave herself. It's not easy to undo twenty-four years of living with liberal artists. She needs to know what it means to be with a real man, and she'll thank me in the end. Gwen will do anything, and I mean *anything* to get me back."

"Why are you like this, Marcus? Wouldn't you prefer to be loved by a woman who loved you for you– not because she's afraid of you?"

"There's nothing wrong with demanding my woman to improve herself. A man has to look out for himself, and that means keeping his wife in tow. But you wouldn't understand. You're an *artist,* a *genius* and so everyone breaks their back to please you. Well, I live in the real world. In my world, there are real men and there are wussies who can't control their women. My father never could, so my mother was a broken, but uncontrollably self-indulgent house-whore because of it. My wife and my daughter are going to be different." (The parole board has denied your petition yet again, Charles)

"By tomorrow morning, one of us will be out there with Gwen!"

"You'll only make it worse for her. She'll have to answer to me. All we want is your money, not you."

"We'll see."

When we parted, he shook my hand and smiled his smile, like we were old friends. I walked around the streets for a while trying to decide what to do. The obvious thing was to call Dara and have her go to Gwen, but I'd suffered through the pain of my bluff, and didn't want to give in by calling her again, even if it meant that I was acting more like Marcus than I dared to contemplate. Nothing would get resolved with Dara unless she knew that I was serious. But Gwen shouldn't have to continue to suffer because her parents were immature idiots. She needed love and support more than money right now. It looked like I was the only one available to go. Fuck what Marcus thought. Fuck what Dara would think. Even fuck what Gwen thought she wanted!

I made reservations for a night flight and a room at a hotel as close as the travel agent could find to the address Marcus had reluctantly given me. Going back to Northport made no sense, so I bought some necessities and a small carry-on bag for the trip, then called Ellen at work to ask if I could stay with her after work until it was time to go to the airport. She suggested that I stop at her office to get her keys and wait for her at her apartment.

To thank her, I prepared dinner at her apartment. By the time the meal was ready, Ellen had arrived.

"Do you want me to come with you?" she asked when she heard about my conversation with Marcus, and my plans.

"Ellen, this is Dara's daughter. How appropriate would that be?"

"Oh yeah, Dara." She fell silent.

"I have a niece in Salem," she said, a moment later. "Is that anywhere nearby? I could stay with her."

"How old?"

"What?"

"Your niece."

"Early twenties. Why?"

"Does she have a job?"

"She teaches first grade. Why, again?"

"Can we call her? Do you have her number? What's her name? Is she nice?"

"Slow down, Leo. You're ranting. Tell me, slowly, what you're talking about."

"She might know someone who could help Gwen take care of Carrie for a while so Gwen can deal with her own problems more easily. Gwen is just outside Salem."

Ellen's niece was unable to do it herself because she was taking graduate courses, but suggested a teacher friend who was working as a temp all summer for the money. I told Ellen's niece to offer her friend two hundred dollars a day and expenses to work for me, and to leave her name and phone number at the Salem airport if she wanted the job. Ellen had become an invaluable resource in the Marcus/Gwen saga.

Though she had to work the next day and the flight was at midnight, Ellen insisted upon accompanying me to the airport. We spent the remaining time with our clothes on, discussing the various ways I should approach Gwen. The most important thing was to follow Gwen's lead, and do whatever was needed.

Would Gwen receive me well, would I be able to help at all, would Gwen listen to reason? Although we shared a bottle of champagne during the limo ride, and had another drink at the airport after I had checked in, I still hadn't shaken my anxiety. When Ellen kissed me good-bye at the gate, I felt like I was going off to war.

My flight got me to Salem at five in the morning. Marie, the niece's friend left a message for me– she accepted the job. I took a cab to the hotel, checked in and slept for a few hours. I offered to rent a car, but Marie volunteered her own and picked me up at my hotel at ten that morning. We drove to Gwen's.

Marie got us to Gwen's town, but didn't know how to proceed from there. After inquiring at several gas stations and asking people along the road, we finally managed to locate her.

My traveling companion was warm and charming– the kind of woman you'd want your child to have as a first grade teacher– nice, but not sappy. I filled her in, with admittedly broad strokes, as to where we were going and why. She assured me that I could devote my time to Gwen and that she would see to Carrie for as long as she was needed.

Marie made me feel more optimistic about the trip and my mission.

Chapter 23

The optimism faded during the three minutes between my knock on the door of Gwen's trailer and the moment she opened the door. Other trailers surrounded Gwen's. Although a few were new and shiny, or at least Simonized into a respectable glow, most were dilapidated and unkempt. Litter and discarded car parts lay among the cinder blocks that supported the mobile homes. Elsewhere, cracked barren earth with clumps of yellow-brown weeds separated one home from another.

Gwen's eyes grew wide when she opened the door and saw me. With surprise? Fear? Or relief? Marie slipped past me, wordlessly indicating that she would take Carrie from her mother. Gwen automatically handed her the baby, and Marie walked a short distance away.

My estranged daughter– more correctly, the estranged daughter of my estranged girlfriend– flew into my arms and buried her face in my neck, laughing and crying while grasping me powerfully. I wasn't going to get a cold reception, after all. Gwen didn't look good. Her skin was sallow and her hair was pulled back into a tight ponytail. She had gotten pregnant without having lost the weight from her first pregnancy, and her breasts, which had always been large, were enormous and sagged from their own weight. Rather than a maternity dress, she wore a sixties style peasant dress that was too small and had been washed too many times. Marcus' wife dressed like a hippie?

Every now and then, Gwen disengaged herself and took a half step back from me, crying, "Oh Leo," then came right back into my arms. Fifteen minutes later, after she had calmed down a little, she noticed Marie for the first time.

"Where's my mother? Is she all right?"

"Dara's been very depressed about you, Gwen. She hasn't spoken to me in quite a while. I didn't tell her that I was coming."

"Why *did* you come?"

"About three months ago, I arranged to meet Marcus, by surprise. Ever since then, he has been calling me for lunch every few weeks. He told me, yesterday, that he had left you and Carrie, and that didn't sit well with me. You shouldn't be left alone like this."

"You saw him yesterday?"

"Yes, and don't ask me how he is. He doesn't deserve for you to care."

"I love him, Leo."

"Why?"

"You only know one side of him. He can be tender and loving."

"When you've behaved? Come on, Gwen, you're smarter than that. He doesn't respect you, and I doubt that he loves you. Marcus has given me a pretty good idea of how he treats you. You're just property to him. Chattel. Get over him. Move on."

"You of all people should understand. When was the last time you were with my mother?"

"Pretty much not since you left New York."

"And do you still love her? Why don't you get over her? Why don't you move on?"

"Are you really comparing Dara to Marcus? It won't hold up on any level."

"Marcus and I love each other. He's my man!"

"No, he's your master, and you're little more than his slave. It's time to stop kissing the whip."

Gwen was very upset, so I backed off. She had to nurse Carrie and invited us all inside. Carrie was being weaned in anticipation of the next baby, but Gwen didn't have the heart to completely deny her. She felt guilty about the life into which Carrie had been brought.

Inside, the trailer was a sordid hell– tiny and dark and smelled of old cooking and stale tobacco smoke. Filled with lifeless furniture and strewn with toys and clothes, the squalor was dense. If you lived here, there was no glimpsing a happier future. Gwen's home was a refuge for despair.

While Gwen fed Carrie, I urged her to leave the trailer camp for a few days– she couldn't think clearly while she was there. My only hope, and her only hope, was to get her away from that hole.

"What do you do here?"

"Taking care of Carrie takes most of my time. I get tired pretty easily, so I rest when I can. Marcus doesn't like me to go out, so I don't get to the library anymore, and, anyway, I don't have a car. My neighbor, Alice, brings me books when Marcus isn't here. Marcus thinks she's a bad influence, so she stays away when he's around."

"Well, it's time for a little R&R. Marie's going to help you with Carrie, and I'm going to spoil and pamper you like you haven't been treated for a long time. I'll book us all rooms at my hotel, and we'll relax and buy you some nice things, and have dinner out, and whatever else we can think of."

"I can't. What if Marcus comes while I'm gone?"

"He won't. He's with his girlfriend, and even if he does, so what?"

"He'll punish me. For some reason, he particularly hates you."

"He only punishes you because you let him– he's just a bully. Stand up to him and you'll be surprised how easy it is. You're not alone. Every city and town has a place where battered women, women like you, can go for help and shelter. We're leaving here. Take whatever you'll need for you and Carrie for tonight. Anything else, we'll get in Salem."

Gwen was used to doing what she was told, and we were ready to go in an hour. I had used the time to get two additional and adjoining rooms for Gwen and Marie not far from my own. Just before we left, Gwen insisted that she tell her friend Alice that she was going away for a few days. I made her promise not to tell her where.

We settled in. Once Gwen relaxed a little in the cocoon that Marie and I spun for her, she started to overflow with her story. Marie played with Carrie in one room, and Gwen and I sat in the other while she talked. And talked and talked and talked. By her account– mitigated only formally by an occasional interjection of something positive about Marcus– she had spent her married life terrorized.

The way she described him, Marcus was a sadistic psychotic who brutalized her emotionally, physically and sexually. She was virtually held prisoner, though Marcus threw her crumbs of affection as long as she did his bidding. Each story nauseated me more than the previous one, and I had to make her stop, that first night, long before she was finished. How Gwen could experience the things

Marcus had done and still be willing to stay around for more amazed me. This was a young woman who had grown up around Dara and me.

And speaking of Dara . . .

"Gwen, we've got to take a stop, here. Your story is overwhelming, and I need a rest. Why don't you call Dara? It would help her a lot just to hear from you."

"Do I have to?"

"I'm not Marcus. You don't have to do anything you don't want to do. But Dara's not Marcus either. You may think she's overbearing, but she's trying. And it's purely out of love."

Gwen did call, and got Dara's machine like all the rest of us. We had dinner in the hotel restaurant, then returned to the rooms where Gwen continued her story. At ten o'clock, just when I needed another break from the Marcus tales, the phone rang.

No one but Dara was supposed to know that we were at that hotel. I was closest to the phone and, anyway, if it was Dara, I wanted to talk to her first. She had to be told about Gwen's initial response to my visit, and urged to use restraint when she spoke to her daughter. But I was also doing it for my own needs. This could be considered Dara calling me first, and I wouldn't have to worry about sustaining my bluff any longer.

"Hello."

"Leo?"

"Yes, Dara."

"You bastard!"

"And a pleasant good evening to you, too."

"You could have called me. Let me know you were going out there."

"I told you I wouldn't call again." Silence.

"You're a bastard anyway."

"I know. I'm just the worst possible person in the world for coming out here to help Gwen. You remember Gwen, don't you? You know, the daughter who has gotten you so emotionally distraught that you can't talk to me anymore? I wish you didn't think that I'm a bastard, but then, there's a lot of things I wish you didn't think."

"I can't be anything else than who I am."

"No one knows who you are more than I do. This is not Dara."

"Is Gwen there?" She chose to ignore me. Gwen was right beside me, but wasn't paying attention to what I said to Dara.

"Can the new Dara be gentle?"

"Just get her for me."

"Nice chatting with you, too. Here's Gwen."

Chapter 24

Things were going well. Gwen got more relaxed every day. She even smiled, now. Her interaction with Carrie was voluntary and positive. Before, she had merely provided for her needs. We went to movies and galleries, and Gwen did more than her share of shopping. I was getting ready to talk to her about returning East with me.

Marie was great– great with Carrie, great with Gwen and a tremendous help to me, but I was confused about our relationship. I was her boss, yet she was teaching me how to care for Carrie. She was always in a good mood and always smiling. I didn't know if her warmth toward me was just her overall friendliness or something else.

She was Gwen's age, so it was hard to imagine that she was attracted to me. Marie wasn't beautiful, but pretty enough, and had a thin, muscular body . What were my intentions?

We were playing house with Leo as the father figure, Marie as the mother and Carrie as a very convincing baby. Gwen was my slightly wayward daughter from a previous marriage. No wonder I was confused. To think of Marie as a potential lover was ridiculous, but I was desperately Dara-less, so willing to try on other women to attempt to lessen my need for the woman I really wanted.

Marie brought the situation into perspective when she asked to have some free time to spend with her boyfriend. He was coming home from the Navy for the weekend. Someone needed to clear the confusion, and I was glad Marie had done so, and done it before I embarrassed myself and lost her help. As her reward for saving me from my own foolishness, I not only gave her the time, but told her to invite him to stay with her at the hotel if she chose to. She accepted at once.

On Thursday morning, Marie called my room to say that she had been awakened by Carrie's wails in the next room. When her knocks weren't answered, she went in and found Carrie alone, wet and hungry with Gwen nowhere to be found. On Friday, with no word from Gwen, I moved into Gwen's room to do most of the caring for Carrie while Marie spent time with her boyfriend.

Spending uninterrupted time with my— would-be-if-only-I-was-talking-to-her-grandmother— granddaughter was a wonderful experience, and I didn't mind Carrie's ever present demands. Being needed so much was exciting. I told Marie that I wouldn't need her at all for the weekend, and to enjoy herself with her boyfriend.

There was a knock on my door late Sunday afternoon. At first, I thought it was Marie knocking on the connecting door, but when I opened my side, the other door was locked. Marie was with her boyfriend. A key turned in the hall door lock and the next thing I knew, Gwen was pushed into the room by an enraged Marcus.

The right side of Gwen's face was swollen and bruised, and her right eye was barely open. I opened my arms to Gwen, but she stayed back and made no attempt to go to Carrie. Gwen looked mentally beaten, as well.

"I told you it would make things worse for Gwen if you came out here."

"Does it make you feel like a real man to beat a pregnant woman? Does it get you hard?"

"Shut up, Leo!"

"What's the matter? Don't you like what I'm saying? Tell me, Marcus, what's it like to punch a soft, unprotected pregnant woman who won't defend herself? A woman who loves you too much to even try to stop you. Is that what love is to you, brutality and pain?"

"SHUT UP!"

"What are you thinking? Or is thought too much for you? They say that wife-beaters are impotent if they're not inflicting pain. Is that it?"

"I want my baby girl. Just shut up and hand her over. She's mine!"

"Not anymore, schmuck. I'm not going to let you abuse her, too. People aren't property. Not wives. Not children. And definitely not Carrie. You want her, get a good lawyer because Dara and I are taking you two to court to gain custody. If Gwen can't do what's right for Carrie by dumping you, she doesn't deserve Carrie, either."

"Watch it, you're talking about my wife."

"No I'm talking about your slave and your whipping post. What's the matter, am I devaluing your portfolio?"

"Gwen came back to me on her own free will after you tried to bribe her away. She's an adult and makes her own choices– and you have no right to take Carrie."

"Well, too bad then. I'm taking her back to Dara, anyway. If you try to stop me, I'll have every policeman in Oregon on your ass. Now run along, Marcus, and go plan your next psychotic break. Gwen, if you're smart, you'll stay with us."

Marcus lost it.

"You motherfucking scumbag. All of a sudden you're the knight in shining armor. Where were you all those years when other people were counting on you? (?) Painting pretty little fucking pictures, or fornicating with Gwen's slut mother where all the world can see you? Degenerates like you should be exterminated like the vermin you are. You're not going to corrupt my daughter like you did Gwen.

"And then when reality gets too much for you, you go to sleep for a fucking month. Like a fucking moth in a cocoon. Give me my daughter or I'm going to beat in your shitty little moth brain."

"I don't think so." That could have been my voice. In fact, it should have been my voice. It wasn't.

Steve, Marie's boyfriend. They had both come into my room when the noise level escalated. Steve was young, tall and in perfect shape. He wasn't wearing a shirt and presented an imposing presence. Marcus, in his rage, would certainly have been able to overpower me. But not Steve, and definitely not both of us.

Outnumbered and temporarily stymied, Marcus slammed his fist into the wall, making a hole in the plasterboard. The blow must have hurt him, though he showed no sign of pain.

"I'll be back, pussy, when your bodyguard is gone." He stormed out of the room.

Gwen followed.

"Don't go, Gwen. Please. The man's a brute and he's likely to take out his rage on you. Think about your unborn baby – come home with me, Gwen. Please. We can leave tonight."

"I've got to go, Leo. My husband needs me." She shuffled out, bent and broken.

Marie, Steve and I simultaneously took a deep and troubled breath when Gwen left.

"What are you going to do?" Marie asked.

"Take Carrie to her grandmother. First, I need to speak to a good lawyer. Carrie's not related to me, and I don't want to get arrested for kidnaping her. Do you know anyone? I want to do this right."

Finding a confidence-inspiring lawyer who secured a temporary court order allowing me to take Carrie back to New York, took three days. After booking a flight, I called Dara's machine (the machine and I were getting very close) and left the flight information and the following message.

"Pick us up at the airport, and Carrie can stay with you. But I'm not going to chase you. So, if you're not there, Carrie's going to live with me. And, by the way, she's worth the effort. Even if it means you have to see me."

Marie drove us to the airport and we parted with kisses, hugs and best wishes all around. She'd been a godsend. I couldn't believe I'd almost gotten carried away and come on to her. What was I thinking? Nothing, certainly, that I wanted to remember.

Dara did meet us at the airport. She said very little to me, but the look on her face as she cuddled and cooed to Carrie made my whole trip worthwhile. She looked a lot like the old Dara: happy, confident and definitely in charge.

Grandmother and granddaughter sat together in the back seat on the trip home, citing the safety issue. Totally absorbed with Carrie, Dara spoke very little to me. I didn't fool myself, however, into thinking that she would have talked to me if Carrie hadn't been there. What am I saying? If Carrie hadn't been there, neither would Dara.

Trapped in her own mood and unwilling to cede her self-imposed, introspective, self-destructive exile for the likes of me, Dara never asked me about Gwen and Marcus. She had constructed the tenor of our relationship (threatening the tenure), and she was stuck with it. Absorbed in her misery, she'd forgotten to construct an escape hatch.

Back at Dara's, as I bent over to kiss Carrie good-bye before taking a cab home, Dara briefly placed her hand on my back, but didn't say anything. Breaking the two-hour silence of our mutual stubbornness, I gave Dara a quick rundown of Carrie's routine and left, not knowing when I would see Carrie, or Dara, again.

Chapter 25

The call I had both feared and expected since my return from Oregon came two weeks later. Though expected, it was no less shocking. At least it wasn't an impersonal police call. Marie phoned.

Gwen was in the Intensive Care Unit of the local hospital. The beating Marcus had given her caused the loss of her unborn baby with massive hemorrhaging that had left her in shock. Attendants in the Emergency Room had found her dumped at the door by *person or persons unknown.* Gwen had also suffered a concussion and several broken facial bones and ribs. When she was conscious enough to talk, she remembered Marie's name and asked the nurses to call her. That was a few hours before Marie called me.

Marie volunteered to stay with Gwen until either Dara or I got there, so I called Dara at once, and said hello to my friend, the answering machine. In case Dara planned to stay true to her demons, and refused to talk to me, I packed a small bag to make the trip myself. Dara reluctantly opened her door after a few minutes of pounding.

Still unaware of the details of my Oregon trip, Dara was less prepared for the stunning news of Gwen's predicament. She broke through the barrier she had erected between us to learn everything she had missed. I promised to fill her in on the way to the airport. One of us was getting on a flight in a few hours.

"Of course, I'm the one who is going. I just need to pack a few things and find someone to take care of Carrie. How much time do I have?" Vestiges of the old Dara were surfacing.

"We should leave as soon as possible. No more than twenty minutes."

"Will you help, then?"

I looked at her as though she was retarded.

"I didn't mean that, Leo. There's a list of babysitters near the phone in my room. Would you mind calling them while I pack?"

"You pack. I'm taking care of Carrie."

"But you're painting again. She'll be a nuisance. You know how much attention she requires."

"This is more important than what I'm doing." Painting endless pictures of you, is what I thought, but didn't say. "Besides, I miss her."

"I'll help you get her crib and stuff into your car. She *will* be better off with you."

"We don't have the time. Besides, she's been moved around enough. The best thing is for me to stay here with her while you're gone."

Silence.

"What's the matter, are you afraid of letting me stay here? I promise I won't read your mail or snoop through your things– though I'm probably not above rummaging through your underwear drawer and wearing a pair of your panties to bed."

"I'm not afraid of you, Leo. You won't understand this, but I love you as much as I ever did. Maybe more."

"Well, then, you need some work on how you show it."

"I've taken your advice– new doctor, medication. I'm getting there."

Carrie and I drove Dara to the airport. She hugged and kissed Carrie at the gate, but turned away when I tried to kiss her good-bye. I struggled to endure one more act of rejection as I plaintively watched her board the plane.

"She really needs to learn how to show it better," I mumbled to the sleeping Carrie.

Chapter 26

There was a note from Marie, which Dara found when she arrived at the hospital in Salem, directly from the airport, at seven in the morning. Marie had gone home to get some sleep, but would be back between nine and ten. Dara also found Gwen, bruised and swollen, and barely responsive.

The young woman appeared barely human to her own mother. Her body was swollen, yet sagged with blue and yellow bruises overlying dull, ghostly white skin. Gwen somehow recognized Dara, smiling weakly as tears came to her eyes, but when she tried to speak, her voice came out as a slurred moan.

"It's okay Gwen. I'm here now. No one is ever going to hurt you again. Just rest and let yourself heal."

Dara tried to remain calm and not burst into tears herself. While she'd been caught up in her orgy of self-loathing and self-inflicted pain, Gwen was facing real issues and real danger. The mother had been so busy immersing herself in guilt over her past failures with Gwen that she'd been unavailable to help her daughter in the present. Twice, I had to be called instead of Dara.

We weren't people who attempted to control one another. In all the years I've known Dara, she has never tried to change a single thing about me. Her need to control was confined to her work, and to Gwen.

Situations that arose were handled by the first one on the scene. There had been no turf wars, not even over Gwen. Dara was supposedly spending all her time consumed with her concerns about Gwen, while I was immersed in painting. Yet, both times that Gwen needed immediate help, I was there and Dara had been inaccessible—shielded from reality by her damn answering machine.

A nurse came over to introduce herself, and was relieved to learn that Dara was Gwen's mother. Gwen needed an ally and an advocate. She needed more TLC than the nurses, dedicated as they were, could give her. Despite Gwen's reluctance to talk about what had happened, her circumstances were no mystery to any of the medical personnel. Tragically, Gwen's plight was too common an occurrence.

"I know she must look awful to you, but those are just bruises and swelling that will heal. Gwen's almost stable enough to be transferred out of the ICU. With you here, her transfer to a regular room can be accelerated."

"I'd like her to stay here as long as possible. Even if it means paying for it myself."

"We need the beds for seriously ill patients. It's not a matter of paying for it. Fortunately, Gwen is doing well and has outgrown us. She'll be fine on a regular floor."

Dara's eyes glowed with power and assurance. These were the eyes of the old Dara, the eyes that appeared in my paintings. Those eyes tolerated no disagreement. They were the eyes with which I had fallen in love.

"I'll see to that. Right now, I want to speak to her doctor."

"Gwen doesn't have a specific doctor. She was more or less dumped at the hospital and is being taken care of by the resident surgical staff. There was the question of insurance and . . ."

"Get me the chief resident, then."

"I'm not sure if Dr. Fields is available. I haven't seen him yet today. He may be in surgery."

"I want to see him as soon as he's free. If he remains unavailable, I'll want to see the hospital administrator, or the chief of the residency program."

When Dara decided to take charge, no one was a match for her. Her voice commanded, her eyes left no room in this universe to disobey.

"I'll page Dr. Fields. That's all I can do. The residents make rounds around eight, so they should be here soon."

"Thanks. I don't mean to be difficult, I'm just a very worried mother." Dara didn't want the nurse to be annoyed by her, and subconsciously take it out on Gwen.

"I understand that this is very stressful for you. I'll speak to Dr. Fields."

The residents did come by as promised. They went from patient to patient muttering the mumbo jumbo of doctors that was created, Dara suspected, to keep patients and their families at a distance. When they got to Gwen's bed, they completely ignored Dara and continued as before.

"Which one of you is Dr. Fields?"

"I am. And you are?"

"Dara Harrington, Gwen's mother." Dara extended her hand and Dr. Fields gave it a perfunctory shake. "I'd like to talk to you about Gwen."

"I won't be able to, right now. As soon as we finish rounds, I have to get to the operating room." Dr. Fields was haughty and full of himself. He had failed to make eye contact with Dara, a sin he would come to regret.

"Okay, then when can I expect you?"

"I can't promise a time. I'm very busy today."

"What can you possibly be busy with that doesn't include the proper care of your patients?"

"I have priorities. Emergencies. Very sick patients. I'm sorry, but I'll get to you when I can."

"I don't think so. What is the name of your superior?" Dara had caught the attention of the other residents.

Dr. Fields must have been an unbearable chief resident. The others enjoyed seeing Dara make him squirm.

"I suppose I can make some time at about one."

"One o'clock, then. And please let me know if you're going to be late. I get ornery if I'm kept waiting." Several residents were openly smirking. They moved on.

Dara went for coffee. By the time she returned, so had Marie.

The two women had neither met nor spoken before. Marie was too nice for that to ever matter to her, and Dara was too preoccupied with Gwen to stop to appraise Marie. Marie filled Dara in on my trip to Oregon. Dara still hadn't met Marcus, so when Marie told her how he had burst into the room behind an obviously beaten Gwen, and demanded Carrie during a verbal assault directed at me, Dara was unnerved.

"Would you mind if I continue to visit Gwen now that you're here? I felt so sorry for Gwen while we were all living together, and I can't stop thinking about the way she looked that day after Marcus had beaten her. I just want to see her get better." Dara liked Marie before she'd had the chance to consider an alternative.

"Of course. That's so nice of you. And it will be a help to me, too. I think I'm going to be here for a while and it will give me someone to talk with. Come whenever you like."

A few days later, Gwen was transferred to a private room. Dr. Fields had been scrupulously punctual to his appointment with Dara. She asked the doctor to tell her Gwen's most pressing problem.

"She's mostly sore and bruised. Her concussion seems to be resolved. Gwen's ribs will heal on their own, and the facial fractures have been surgically repaired– they're healing nicely. Her only significant remaining problems are anemia and her full recovery from the surgery required to repair her uterus." Despite a lot of transfusions, Gwen was still anemic from the traumatic miscarriage and her ruptured womb.

"Thank you, doctor. That wasn't so difficult, was it?"

Based on the resident's report, Gwen called the chief of Gynecology and asked him to recommend a doctor to follow Gwen. She selected the one woman on the list, and asked her to take over Gwen's care. She also called Marcus' company to straighten out the insurance information. During the call, she learned that Marcus had been "let go" several weeks before– which meant that he'd been fired before the last time we had lunch– and it wasn't clear if Gwen was actually covered.

Dara finally remembered to call home to check on Carrie, and not, I supposed, to talk to me. Carrie and I were getting along great. She was a happy, even-tempered little girl who showed no signs of damage from her home life. The tiny little girl who was my only link to the two women who mattered most to me cooed and laughed, and made no more demands than any other ten-month-old. I'd missed my time away from her, another gripe I had about the way Dara had been treating me. When Carrie started to crawl around the house, I pulled out my old Leica for the first time since my photorealism days.

To add to my long list of grievances, Dara hadn't given me a report about Gwen as soon as she'd arrived in Oregon. That was plain mean of her. So when Dara first called, I gave her a taste of herself, and let her talk to her answering machine. The frustration in her voice as she insisted that I pick up the phone satisfied me. Though it was childish of me, I let her go on until she finally hung up.

Gwen was getting stronger, ready to leave the hospital in a few days, though her doctors advised against traveling for at least another week. In anticipation, Dara moved out of her hotel and booked two rooms at another hotel under an alias. She suspected that Marcus was lurking around somewhere nearby, and wanted to avoid a confrontation– for both Gwen and herself– with the deranged man.

Dara told no one where they were going, not even Gwen. The security aspect of her plan was a good idea, but if something awful happened, hiding incognito prevented anyone from finding out. Since she hadn't voluntarily called me in months, further silence wouldn't alarm me. With no way to contact *her*, I wouldn't even try.

By the time she called again, the need to punish her was gone.

"I'm back."

"At the airport?"

"No, Leo, I mean I'm *back* back."

"How do you know? How do you know if it's for real? I mean, you're there, three thousand miles from the reality that is Leo Schultz. You may come home and realize you just thought you were back."

"Leo, I know."

"It's been a long time. I need to be sure."

"Too long. Am I too late?" The way she said those words made me sure.

"No, of course not. Never. It just seems like a lifetime. A horrible, awful lifetime."

"I'm sorry, Leo, so terribly sorry. This isn't the first time I've had to apologize to you for being a self-absorbed loser. Why do you even like me?"

"Like painting. I have no choice. It's what I do. I paint and I love you. Paint. Love. That's who I am. Usually, you're exceedingly loveable. I've missed you so much."

"I've missed you too. I just couldn't pull myself out of the abyss I was in. After a while I forgot the way back to you. I couldn't figure out the first step."

"But you're back now?"

"I'm back. I'm really back."

"Carrie and I will be there tomorrow. Do you need anything?"

"You can't come. We're trying to hide from Marcus. If you come, it may attract attention and we'll be home in four or five days. By the way, Marcus lost his job."

"No surprise, he's way out of control. Totally rabid. Don't let Gwen out of your sight. She may go to him again."

"She's in no shape to do that, but I'll watch her. Marie filled me in on most of the details, and Gwen added some others. She hasn't accepted losing the baby, or that she can never have another one.

"Did you talk with her about it?"

"I'm going to wait. She's got enough to sort through. How's Carrie?"

"Adorable and crawling. I'm totally in her power to do with as she pleases."

"Don't spoil her too much. We have to live with her."

"I'll try, but she's irresistible."

"I'll call you. Answer."

"I will, now that I know the person I'm talking to. Tell Gwen I love her."

"I'll tell her, but I think she already knows that. And . . . Leo?"

"What?"

"I never, for a second, stopped loving you. Though it must have looked that way to you, I never did. I love you so much."

"We have a lot to talk about when you get home. Right now, just take care of yourself and Gwen. If you even get a whiff of Marcus, call the police. Don't take any chances. You can see for yourself that he's very dangerous. I'll speak to you soon. Bye."

"I'll call you tomorrow."

When I hung up, my body withered from exhaustion. Not like a fugue was coming on, my emotional being had been savaged just as badly as Marcus had brutalized Gwen. Though having Dara back was the answer to months of prayer, I was upset, too, that she could turn it off and on so easily. The next time something happened to Gwen, and something further was bound to happen to her, which of Dara's alternate personalities would I encounter?

Dara had issues– unresolved issues that went back to her childhood and her feelings about her own mother. Whatever the other woman had been– cold hearted? bitch? scapegoat?– whatever she'd done, I was dealing with it now.

Leo Schultz painted, he didn't psychoanalyze. I had no therapeutic talent, but I would insist (insist? to Dara?) that Dara continue with whomever had gotten her this far in her therapy. That was one of the things we would talk about. There was no way I could go through this again, even with Dara.

Was this fair, O Leo of the fugue? Leo who changed his career after each long nap. Leo who couldn't control his own existence was asking, no demanding, that the person he loved most in this world, control hers. Leo who, at times, couldn't put down his paintbrush. This same Leo was asking Dara to put aside her maternal conflicts?

Though the way I painted changed when I awoke from a fugue, my basic personality, or the way I acted toward Dara and others never did. The essential Leo-ness remained constant, only my painting was different.

The moth analogy wasn't quite right. Caterpillars aren't the same as moths. I went into my fugues striped and came out paisley, but I was still the same old moth. So fuck Marcus and fuck his cocoon imagery! Moth!

Justifying my entire existence was comforting, but didn't make the exhaustion go away. I couldn't conceive of putting Dara through what she'd put me through. Not only was I exhausted, but confused. Maybe this would all sort itself out in the morning. Still, whatever neurotic baggage she brought with her, Dara was back. I believed her. For tonight, that was enough.

Carrie was sound asleep when I checked on her before going to bed. Nor did she stir during my three kisses– one for Dara, one for Gwen and one for myself. Then I went to bed.

I tossed in my bed as the unknowns of my future robbed me of needed rest. How were Dara and I going to get over the chasm that had been dug between us? Dara would want to talk through the problem. I wanted to talk too, but what would I say? Many things needed to be said simultaneously: I missed her, I grieved for her, I hated her, I loved her, I needed her, I never wanted to see her again,

I never wanted to leave her side, I love her more than ever, it will never be quite the same together, I depend on her, I'll always be insecure about her. There was no good order to say those things separately. They all had to be said at the same time to convey what I really meant. But then I thought, *calm down Leo, this is Dara. One hug will say it all.* And one good hug is all I would need.

So now to sleep.

No.

Ellen.

What words for Ellen? *Thanks for servicing me while Dara was adrift, but she's back now so I don't need you anymore? Have a nice life. Oh, and I'll call you if Dara and I ever get separated again.*

Ellen had been my friend, my confidante and, don't forget, my lover when I desperately needed all three. Walking away from her now would be a despicable act by a selfish man. Ellen's greatest crime was loving me more than I loved her. Otherwise, she had behaved with grace and candor. Ellen had forgiven me once, and I responded by abusing her again. Was I really any different than Marcus?

Ellen would pretend to be understanding, maybe sympathetic. She had seen my studio–unable, in the end, to resist looking– with its Dara shrine disguised as paintings. We were always both acutely aware that our time together had been for the moment, that we weren't going to last. In my tacky cowardice, I had absolved myself. never misrepresented myself, never deceived her. Ellen would be the first to exonerate me, saying a lot of words with facts to back them. Ellen was never at a loss for words. We'd both pretend, but we'd both know that not a word of it was true.

Ellen was doomed to be hurt again. It was our Sisyphus myth. She would roll me, swollen and helpless, curled up in a fetal ball, up the hill. When we got near the top, I would come barreling down over her, crushing her beneath me. If I hit the bottom, she might offer to roll me up again. How many times could I let that happen?

My sleepless confusion made me wax overly dramatic. Dara's return was an emotional maelstrom, and my psyche was pummeled by the simultaneous love and hate of two women. Worst of all, I was doing to Ellen what Dara had done to me, only I was doing it for keeps. Even though I stayed true to my fundamental self, discarding Ellen wasn't any less unconscionable. Sacrificing Ellen was just as morally corrupt.

I should have never let this happen in the first place, nor abandoned decency for my own selfish and childish needs. Instead, saying those meaningless, self-serving and ridiculous disclaimers was supposed to make it all okay. As if that would make it all right. *But judge, I told him I might end up killing him, and he was okay with that.*

Ellen, Ellen, Ellen. What was I going to say to Ellen?

Finally, sleep. With sleep came dreams –dreams of Ellen and dreams of Dara. Of a girl named Susan whom I thought I had loved in college. And dreams of Sylvie who I still don't know if I had ever loved at all. Gwen and Carrie and the loathsome Marcus entered my dreams, as well. I even dreamed about Marie and Steve although they somehow changed into my mother and father.

The ghosts of my subconscious were still vivid and troubling when I awoke with a headache. There were too many loves squandered and lost to the more potent allure of an empty canvas. If Dara didn't exist, I could survive alone with just the thoughts in my head and a full pallette. People were extraneous. Most of the time, I didn't know how to be around people. Often, like now, I got it all wrong. However, Dara did exist, and that changed everything.

Carrie was singing to herself in the other room, which made me smile. Carrie was there to rescue me from my morbid thoughts– she'd inherited that quality from her grandmother– the ability to make me feel good just being around her.

With Carrie squared away– all set for a morning of play and cuteness– I drank several cups of coffee and then several more while putting off the call to Ellen. Finally, when it came down to adding cowardice to my growing list of despicable personality flaws, and I couldn't put it off any longer, I called. Ellen was out. I left a message. Another machine with which I had a relationship.

"I got your message, Leo," Ellen called back at two that afternoon. "Your tone didn't sound like I'm going to want to hear what you have to say."

"That obvious? Well, I don't want to hear what I'm going to say, either."

"Bad?"

"Bad"

"Dara?"

"Yeah . . ."

"Fuck!"

"Can we do this in person?"

"Right." The word came out harsh and accusatory, or that's the way I was ready to hear it.

Silence.

"Sorry about my outburst." Ellen's voice regained its evenness.

"Hey, what's a *fuck* between friends?"

"That's what I thought at the time."

More silence. I almost lost my resolve, almost backed out.

"I'm so sorry, Ellen. You don't deserve this. I've been unbelievably selfish."

"I hate Dara."

"Don't hate Dara. She hasn't done anything. I'm the one you should hate."

"Okay, then I hate you too, but I still hate Dara. For the way you feel about her. For the way you painted her. No one has ever needed to paint me like that. I'm not even sure that I would want that. But in all my life, I've been the happiest when you're in it, and as long as she's around, you never will be. I hate Dara."

"Ellen, You've been so wonderful, it's just that . . ."

"It's just that DARA! Do you see now why I hate her? If she were a plotting, conniving bitch like I want her to be, I could plot and connive right back and at least have a chance. But she isn't. She's just *Dara*, and somehow that's enough. For her. For you. And it's too much for me."

Ellen was sobbing heavily, filling me with self-loathing and sorrow; filling me with tears myself. But Ellen was right. Dara, even with all our problems, was all I wanted. Dara completed me. Whether it was karma or our own love-struck construction, it was real.

Even while talking to Ellen, I was thinking about Dara– missing Dara, waiting for Dara. In Dara's home, at Dara's desk. With Dara's granddaughter. Mooning over Dara.

For a man who was so engrossed in his painting that women had always been a secondary need, I suddenly– well, not quite so suddenly– found myself enmeshed in an unorthodox triangle with two amazing women. One of them was still on the phone. The wrong one.

"I'm sorry, Leo. I didn't want to cry. I tried." Ellen had gotten control of her sobbing.

"I wish I was with you."

"Don't be crazy. I would have cried. You would have hugged me. It would have felt so good that we would have found ourselves having great sex. Then you would have had to make your speech all over again some other time."

"It wasn't a speech."

"You know what I mean. This kind of news is best delivered over the phone. Then we don't have to look at one another for an awkward few minutes figuring out how to leave gracefully. Until the next time I run into you at an art exhibit, good-bye."

"I don't know what to say."

"Just say *good-bye*. There's one more thing."

"What's that?"

"I hate Dara."

"I know. Goodnight."

"No, good-bye."

"Good-bye."

Click. Whew. My clothes were soaked through with sweat, and the phone was slippery in my hands. My ears rang with Ellen's tears, my vision blurred with my own. The ringing in my ears got louder, and wouldn't stop, I couldn't shut it out, couldn't make it go away. The telephone. It wouldn't stop. The answering machine was turned off because it sometimes took me a long time to get to the phone if I was involved with Carrie. The ringing persisted. Gnawed. I was in no shape to talk to anyone right now. Not anyone. But the phone wouldn't stop. I picked up the receiver, muttering expletives all the while.

Dara spoke my name.

Chapter 27

Not anyone. I rasped out a hello.

"Leo, what's the matter? Is it Carrie?"

"Carrie's fine. Don't make me talk right now. I'll call you back later."

"You can't."

"Oh, right. Call me in an hour, then. Okay?"

"What is it?"

"Not now. I'm hanging up."

I did. She did.

"Leo? What's wrong? Are you sure you're okay?"

"Everything's fine. You just caught me at the worst possible moment."

"What happened?"

"Let's just say that in order to restart with you, I had to end something else."

"Oh."

Silence.

"Are you sure that's what you wanted to do?"

"Yes, definitely yes. Something else we need to talk about, but not now. How's Gwen?"

"Wait. One more question. You sounded really shaken up, before. I'm uneasy about this. Are you sure it's not too late for us? Are you sure you did what you really wanted to do?"

"I never even considered my choice for one second."

"Well then, you're right. We'll talk about it when I get home. Still, though I have no right to say this, it makes me feel a little creepy. Gwen's doing well. She's getting stronger every day, and looks so much better."

"When are you coming home?"

"We see the doctor tomorrow. Probably the next day. Friday."

"Let me know. We'll pick you up."

"Leo?"

"Huh?"

"Can we have the conversation I called to have with you?"

"We agreed to wait until you got home."

"Not that. What I called to say is that I love you. What you just told me, maybe I let you forget that."

"That's not what it was about. I never stopped loving you, either. Knowing you loved me is what made it so frustrating, so senseless."

"I can't wait to see you."

"I've been waiting for months."

"You're making me feel bad."

"I didn't want to get into this now, on the phone. But I mean it. These were the worst months of my life."

"I didn't hurt you on purpose. You of all people. Would you believe me if I said that it hurt me, too, even though I could have stopped it anytime I wanted to?"

"We're three thousand miles apart. Let's save this conversation for when I can look at you, when I can touch you."

"I very much want to touch you, too. It's been so long. I've wasted so much of our time. Don't ever let me do this again. Promise?"

"I wish it were that simple."

"Watch. It's going to get better. You'll see."

"We'll talk when you get home. Right now, I just want to close my eyes and think about you and drift into a dreamless sleep."

"That's really nice. Goodnight, Leo."

Chapter 28

They arrived on Sunday morning. Gwen moved as though wading through glue, barely acknowledging Carrie. Carrie didn't react to her zombie mother, but began talking and cooing as soon as Dara took her from me.

Reluctant to return East with her mother– she wanted to call Marcus to okay it with him– Gwen was home with us against her will.. She didn't, or maybe just didn't want to understand that Marcus had almost killed her and was too dangerous for her to be around. All she wanted was to be with him. There was no getting through to her.

The sudden termination of her pregnancy, the loss of blood, and weeks of IV feeding left Gwen's remaining flesh hanging loosely attached to her prominent bones, and gave her the appearance of being both aged beyond her years and childlike. She looked haggard and was very pale– unattractive and asexual except for the presence of her once ample, but now deflated breasts, which sagged forlornly from her rib cage.

Months had gone by since I had been with Dara for more than a few minutes. She, too, had lost weight but the loss looked good on (off?) her. Her hair was shorter than before, and showed more gray.

Though tired, and strained from the effort of fighting through the exhaustion, her eyes were alive and radiant.

We kissed awkwardly, tentatively, and had to juggle Carrie between us in order to accomplish an only perfunctory hug. I managed the airport chores of collecting the luggage and getting the car. When Carrie fell asleep on the trip back to Northport, the car fell into silence. Gwen continued in her trance-like state, and Dara leaned her head back and closed her eyes.

Carrie transferred to her crib without awakening. Gwen went dutifully to her old room with her silence intact, never greeting me in any way. She had the look, and even the smell, of an institutionalized patient who had severed all links to the here and now. Her thoughts were inaccessible.

Dara declined food or a bath. She struggled out of her clothes and slipped into bed. It didn't seem right for me to help. She was already almost fully asleep when I kissed her lightly on her forehead (now, that felt right) and told her that I would be back first thing in the morning. I never thought she would hear me.

"No, Leo, stay," she muttered sleepily.

I would have demurred, but she was now sound asleep. A part of me wanted to go home. To continue as though nothing had happened between us before we had a chance to talk was wrong. Or at least a chance to hug. Then again, the evil and dangerous Marcus was on the loose, so leaving Gwen, Carrie and Dara unprotected wasn't right either. I wanted to be Conan for my three women. I stayed.

Back in Dara's room, and ready to climb into bed with her, my body recoiled as though repulsed by a field of negative energy. If I got into bed with a naked Dara, no matter that she was sound asleep, all my resolve would dissipate, and our talk would become superfluous. I slept on the couch.

In the morning, as usual, the sound of Carrie calling out for me stirred me from my sleep. Hearing her call, even if it wasn't specifically for me, was a tremendous way to start a day. Carrie and I were well into our morning routine when a sleepy-eyed Dara joined us in the kitchen.

Waking up in the same house with Dara added to the auguries for the day. She crossed the room and we did that misery-ending-homecoming-all-is-forgotten-the-future-is-ours-forget-the-past hug that we had been building toward ever since Dara had called from Oregon to tell me she was back. *Back* back.

The hug lasted quite a while and, in the end, included a measure of chaste caressing. Carrie sang gibberish in the background. Finally, it was time to either throw Dara to the floor and jump on her, or break our embrace. We broke.

Dara wanted to do something grandmotherly for Carrie, but Carrie didn't need anything at the moment, so she poured herself a cup of coffee, and we sat together at the kitchen table while Carrie sat across from us in her highchair. Dara alternated between sipping her coffee and laying her head on my shoulder. Domestic bliss!

"I didn't feel you in bed with me last night."

"I slept on the couch."

"What's wrong?"

"You're kidding, right?"

"I mean, I know what's wrong. You know me, though. I intended to just wish it all away, or make it as though it never happened and start from where we had left off. Forget that I don't deserve it from you, are you going to give me a chance to prove that I've changed?"

"You don't need to prove anything to me. The fact that you're here, that you're back, is good enough for now. Let's not pretend anything, though. We've never done that, so don't let's start. Jumping into bed with you like that, ignoring ten or twelve months of our lives, was too much culture shock for me. I wanted to. I needed to lie next to your naked body, even if you were sleeping, but that would have been wrong, and I've already done too many wrong things, lately."

"So, what now?"

"We talk about this."

"Go ahead. Start."

"Not like that, like we're in front of a judge. Let's just let it happen. Let's not force it."

"I don't know what you want from me."

"This is new territory for me, too. But let's not sit here and present each other with a list of needs and wants, and then hash out the compromises. You know, *I'll be more attentive, if you'll be less demanding.* Stuff like that. What I really want is for our combined us-ness to mutate and grow into a better us-ness."

"I'm sorry that I caused you to lose your mind. Or is it *our* mind?"

"My thoughts have been consumed, for months, searching for the right words to say to you. It turns out that I need to say about a dozen things all at the same time. Any other order won't do. You'd misunderstand, or else I wouldn't be able to make myself clear. That hug said most of what I wanted to say, more simply and more eloquently."

"You're not the only one who has thought about this conversation. There's nothing to say that isn't ridiculous. Explain myself? There is no explanation for my irrational behavior. Apologize? If I did nothing but apologize for the rest of my life, it still wouldn't tell you how sorry I am.. So what's left? I'll tell you. There's only the way I feel about you, and that's everything. You may be hurt, and even angry, and disappointed and freaked out by the last few months, but being close to you, touching you, watching the creases at the corners of your eyes, makes me sure that I didn't destroy our love, didn't irrevocably alter the way we love one another. You're right about the hug. The hug didn't lie."

"That's what I meant. You just said it better. The hug tells us where we are. The talk will come at its own pace and fill in some of the details, the stuff. The talk may be unnecessary, but I'm guessing that we'll want to have it, later. Not all at once. Just as things come up."

"Aren't we talking now?"

"Yeah, but only about talking. We're not doing the talking we're talking about."

"You have lost your mind, haven't you?"

"In a way, I guess I have."

"We've been apart too long."

"Almost a year."

"No, I mean longer than that– forever. We never lived together. That has to stop. I don't want to be away from you any more."

"Really?"

"Yes, really. Why shouldn't we? Don't you want to?"

"It's not that. It's a surprise. I thought you liked separate houses."

"My choice was made a long time ago, and never addressed again. Living apart was just what we did."

"What about Carrie and Gwen? Would Gwen go for it?"

"Gwen is even more out of it than she was as a teenager. Chances are, she won't even notice. Day and night, one day and another don't register with her. As for Carrie, she thrives on you. She loves you the best. What could be bad about an intact family life?"

"Before we get into that, while we're talking, or at least talking about talking, we should talk about Gwen– and her charming husband."

"She doesn't hold Marcus accountable for anything. When I finally told her about losing her baby and that she'd never have any more, her only reaction was that she was afraid of disappointing Marcus. Nothing about her own feelings. Nothing about herself at all. It's scary. All she wants is to go back to that animal."

"She ignored Carrie last night after not seeing her for . . . how long? That saddens me the most. Did she contact Marcus while you were in Oregon?"

"She tried. God knows, she tried. She couldn't find him. Not even at his girlfriend's. That's a whole other story. Evidently he's teaching her an invaluable moral lesson about love and fidelity. Isn't Marcus supposed to be the last Keeper of God's Laws?"

"You haven't met him, Dara. Marcus is totally committed to what he says. And he's totally, and I mean totally, insane."

"How did you sit through those lunches? I would have left with my salad fork sticking out of his forehead."

"Meeting with him was the only way to get any information about him– and about Gwen. I fought the nausea and the rage for Gwen's sake. And I drank large quantities of vodka."

"It should have been me there."

"This time it was me. Next time it will be you."

"There *is* going to be a next time, isn't there?"

"There will be if we don't do something to prevent it. What about therapy?"

"You know how many years of therapy she's had. Therapy hasn't done any good so far, and she's in total denial. Like you said before, she's not aware of what's going on around her. At least she hasn't acknowledged a thing."

"Well then, let's find Marcus and have him killed."

"You're serious, aren't you, Leo?"

"Dead serious."

"Where did that come from?"

"He's not the kind of man you can reason with or threaten. There's no other way to stop him."

"We'd lose Gwen and maybe even Carrie."

"She never has to know. Marcus isn't exactly an upstanding citizen. Any number of accidents could happen. Or he could piss off the wrong people."

"Now *you're* scaring me. How did we get to the point where we're discussing murder so calmly? Promise you won't do anything that will get you in trouble."

"Let's see what develops. We'll save it as a back-up plan, as a last resort. The only thing we can hope for is that Marcus takes a magic pill that turns him into a sane, caring, sensitive father and husband."

After all our talking and after showering, getting dressed, and caring for Carrie, it was almost noon, and Gwen still hadn't stirred. Dara had been checking on her from time to time.

We talked about a lot of collateral issues. Dara had taken an extended leave of absence from work and it was time for her to go back to work, or make the decision to leave the agency. Though Carrie and Gwen needed her at home, Dara missed her work. Retirement, whether temporary or permanent, wasn't an issue that could, or should, be decided in one conversation. I couldn't imagine Dara not working.

We returned to the subject of moving in together. Once we said the words, living apart was no longer feasible. We should have moved in together years and years before. All that was left, were the particulars.

"I should move here. You've created this house with so much love and care that I can't imagine you walking away from it."

"You mean you intend to live more than fifty feet from your studio? You'd go mad! I always suspected that was the real reason why you broke up with Sylvie. Besides, this house isn't big enough for the four of us, especially when Carrie gets a little older. Your place is a lot bigger, and you have all that extra land in case we need to expand.

"Don't forget that I decorated your house too, and I can bring all the things that really matter with me."

Before things went any further, I wanted to tell Dara about Ellen. Not that it would matter, but I wanted to give Dara the option of it mattering. Coward that I am, though, I convinced myself that bringing it up too soon, it would give it greater importance than it deserved, and relished that workable pretense to avoid coming clean.

The guilt about my treatment of Ellen, and the guilt about not telling Dara bubbled inside of me, so I couldn't contain my confession for too long. Dara already knew that there had been someone. She just didn't know who.

Chapter 29

Though anxious to make love, circumstances and timing got in our way for a few days. With sex so imminent, there was no way to continue to defer telling Dara about Ellen. I brought it up without introduction or warning while Dara was making lunch for Carrie.

"Remember Ellen?"

"Your Ellen?"

"Yes, Ellen Sinclair."

"I haven't thought about her in years."

"I ran into her."

"Where?"

"At an art gallery in Soho. I'll have to tell you what I was doing there,some other time"

"When?"

"When I was at my most desperate, most lonely and most miserable point." There, I had done it! Sort of.

"Oh!" Dara stopped spooning baby food into Carrie's tray, and turned to face me.

"How is she?" The muscles of her jaw clenched saying the words.

"That's not what you want to ask."

"If I have to ask, then I know the answer."

"Ellen helped me out when I needed a friend."

"And a lover?"

"And a lover. But never as a replacement for you. As you'll recall, you were mysteriously inaccessible to me."

"So, you and Ellen? That's all my fault?"

"Of course not. I take full responsibility. In fact, I feel terribly guilty about using her, even though I made it perfectly clear that I was still waiting for you. We pretended we knew what we were doing."

"Are you guilty about being unfaithful to me?"

"No. As self-serving as that is, I never abandoned you, never left you for another woman– not in the cosmic sense at least– even though I physically cheated on you. There simply isn't any choice between you and anyone else."

"And so, when I called you that night, you had just told Ellen that it was over?"

"I'm not proud of myself. Even though we had established the ground rules ahead of time, and never pretended that our relationship was going anywhere, it wasn't easy breaking up with her. That was the second time I had done it. Ellen has never been anything but good to me. She's the one who got me in touch with Marcus. She was very supportive when I went to Oregon, and she's the one who hooked me up with Marie. I'm not proud of myself."

"That's another thing I've been wondering about. You and Marie."

"Nothing happened between me and Marie. I won't pretend it never occurred to me. I would guess, however, that it never occurred to her."

"So you feel guilty about what you did to Ellen, but not what you were doing to me? What did Ellen do when you told her? What did she say?"

"Ellen sensed it coming, so she wouldn't meet with me; made me do it over the telephone. She cried a little. As for what she said, if I may quote her directly, *I hate Dara* "

"She said that?"

"A few times."

"Thanks. I need fewer friends."

I looked at Dara carefully, looked deep into her eyes– a dangerous thing to do, you could get consumed and never be seen again after doing that. She looked back. Her gaze seared through to my brain. But I lived, so I knew it would be all right.

"Don't ever make the mistake of thinking Ellen could be your friend," I ventured.

"Ellen doesn't matter. I'm almost glad that there was someone looking after you. Almost. And I feel sorry for Ellen. I don't wish her any ill will, but I have some questions."

"Go ahead. No secrets."

"Why does she hate me? Aren't you the one she should hate?"

"She said that if you were a scheming bitch, she could deal with you, and try to fight back. But I prefer you just because you're you, and she never had a chance– not the first time, not now. She knows that I could never love her the way I lone you.."

"Did you see her a lot?"

"Mostly on weekends. We were both working. You know how I get. And there was the distance."

"What are you working on now?"

"You."

"Still?"

"Still. I've been immersed in Dara. Wallowing in Dara. Painting you was the only way I could keep you near me. Painting you was something I couldn't stop myself from doing– kind of like masturbation. My obsession was more intense than ever before because it was more than about painting. I was grieving your loss in the way I know how to do best. The sickness and irony of the situation didn't escape me. I was carrying on with Ellen while I was drowning in you."

"What did Ellen think?"

"That was part of our charade of being sophisticated and mature. You know, *let's enjoy it while we can since we know this is only temporary* crap. She knew about the paintings– despite my attempt to keep them separate from her. Eventually, she insisted on seeing them."

"Wow!"

"Wow is right."

"And the sex? How was the sex?"

"Good."

"Good or great?"

"Sometimes great. Always good."

"Does she do things you wish I would do? What did you two do together?"

"You're acting like a girl who has just discovered that her first lover used to have another girlfriend."

"You said, *no secrets.* "

"What we did isn't a secret, just irrelevant."

"I want to know, anyway."

"Why?"

"I just do . . . I want to know what I should do. I want to be everyone and everything for you."

"Dara, I don't want everyone and everything. All you have to do is be Dara, that's all it ever took. I've been telling you the same thing since we met."

But Dara persisted, and she got the whole catalogue, every detail and nuance, every flesh-smearing, as well as elegant plie of our erotic ballet delivered, I must admit, with a malicious and perverse glee. Dara got overkill long before I was finished. However, she had committed herself to the whole recital and didn't ask me to stop.

When Carrie got impatient for her lunch, we busied ourselves attending to her. After lunch, Gwen was still not awake, so Dara went upstairs to awaken her. She was gone a long time.

Gwen had awakened easily enough, but needed convincing to get out of bed. An hour later, she finally came downstairs, tendered a listless nod in the general direction of the three of us, who were playing on the living room floor, and sank into an armchair. The doctor had stressed the need for Gwen to eat well, so Dara made her toast and coffee which Gwen only nibbled and sipped when it was set before her.

"What would you like to do today, Gwen?" Dara sounded like a matron in a grade B movie about a nursing home.

"You won't let me."

"You tried, Gwen. You don't even know where Marcus is, or how to contact him. Even though he can guess where you are, he hasn't called you."

"He's mad at me."

"You mean because he only killed the baby and not you when he beat you? I know that would piss me off."

Dara was merciless, perhaps taking unfair advantage. Gwen was too weak to sustain a protest, and she was, for all practical purposes, stranded with Dara.

"You don't understand Marcus."

"You're right," I joined in, "we don't understand Marcus. Why don't you help us to understand him? Explain about you and Marcus."

"You don't want to understand, you two, you just want to hate him. Marcus isn't an ordinary man, he shouldn't be judged by ordinary standards."

"What makes him not ordinary?"

"I'm too tired to argue with you, Leo. Can't you leave me alone?"

"I will. But I do want to understand all this. So whenever you're ready to talk, I want to listen."

"You're mocking me."

"No, I'm loving you."

"If you loved me, you'd let go. Both of you."

There was no legitimate response to her argument. Of course, parents should let go of their adult children. But should a parent let go if his child were hanging over an abyss? And who's to judge if it *is* an abyss? Parents can always make a compelling case why, in this particular instance, it's appropriate for their child's benefit, to hold on: *I know he claims he loves her, but she's stupid, ugly, divorced, not* (fill in your favorite religion*), pregnant, from the wrong family, a slut, from the wrong side of the tracks, too tall, too fat, not our kind.*

While I pondered all this in silence, Dara sat across from me, fuming. She knew better than to say anything negative about Marcus, but she was having trouble containing herself, so settled for eye contact with me, and a mute exchange of exasperation.

The post-beating Gwen was like the pre-Marcus Gwen except that she didn't look as good. After a few days of Dara's tlc, even that had changed. Her skin took on some color, and her shoulders became less hunched. She slipped back into the apathetic, lifeless Gwen who had been a huge frustration for us, but toward whom we'd had a recent nostalgia– we preferred a vapid and safe Gwen to a terrified and threatened Gwen.

Our little family settled into a domestic routine of sorts. Dara was working again and getting more and more involved. Even though she was only working three times a week, she began spending longer and longer hours away from the house. Ten years of aging vanished from her face as soon as she returned to her job.

I was painting feverishly. The entire Dara cycle was conceived as a single event, so I had known exactly what I was going to paint from the moment I began. But the impetus had been my misery and my separation from Dara. Now that the real Dara had returned to me, I wanted to finish before the fury turned to sentimentality.

We, too, had reverted to form, having sex in a very hazy and unfocused way. We came to bed exhausted and melted into the us for a few minutes before falling into a deep, if troubled, sleep. Gwen was not right, and Marcus always loomed on the horizon. Our sex was more mutual reaffirmation than passion.

Gwen spent perhaps fifteen seconds a day talking to Carrie, but lost interest quickly and turned away. Despite our heavy work loads, Dara and I spent as much time as we could with the adorable child– I got her up in the morning and stayed with her until she was well into her morning play, then Dara sneaked home at lunch, and we'd be with her from suppertime until her bedtime. During the day, we had a group of great babysitters who cared for Carrie at Dara's house according to some rotation that only Dara grasped.

On a Saturday morning, two weeks after Dara had returned, the front door to my studio opened. I kept the doors locked because I didn't always hear people coming into the house when I was deep into a painting and had music playing. That morning, the radio was off because the day was so beautiful that I had opened up all the windows and was painting to the sound of the birds and the breeze-blown trees.

Dara was the only one who had a key, but she never interrupted me while I was working. If there was an emergency at home, she would have called, not come over. Although her arrival seemed odd because Dara had been planning to spend the day with Carrie and maybe Gwen, I kept on painting. If it was Dara, I would know soon enough. If it was somebody else, I wasn't sure if I wanted to know.

Dara walked into the studio a few minutes later, carrying a bucket of champagne and two glasses. She didn't exactly greet me. Her first words were:

"Show me."

The painting on my easel– Dara on the day she had refused to go to Paris with me– was already visible to her. So far, only the outline of her head and her mouth were completed– enough to convey the expression of contempt and dismissal I had encountered that morning.

"Take it from me, as a friend, don't have anything to do with that person."

"I didn't. For a long time. I couldn't. I wasn't allowed."

"Did I really look like that?"

"Only on your good days. But, you're taking this out of context. You've got to see them all together."

"That's why I barged in. Show me."

I put the paintings away before I moved into your house when you went to Oregon. Before that, they were all out, everywhere, surrounding me. I'll show you. While I'm doing that, why don't you open the champagne. I assume that's champagne."

"Can't I help you?"

"I want you to get the full impact of them all at once."

"Should I be frightened?"

"No, honored. They're all of you as seen through my eyes– and you know how I feel about you."

"I can tell from the one on the easel."

"They're honest and no one is perfect. But they all have love in them. If I didn't love you so much, you wouldn't have looked like that to me that day."

Twenty minutes later, the paintings were arranged around my studio. Dara was well into the champagne by then. She handed me a glass and went to look, spending a lot of time with each painting; sometimes going back to one she'd already looked at to look again. No one, not Mo or Barbara or Lee, none of the art critics and none of my artist friends understood my paintings like Dara did. Intuitively, but critically, she could tell exactly why I had painted what I had painted. She had spent extra time on each of the nudes and had gone back, several times, to the one that depicted the first time I had seen her naked.

When she was done, and it had taken more than two hours and several trips by me to the kitchen for more champagne, we sat on the couch with our glasses full again. While I sprawled, Dara sat silent for a long time with her back straight, her eyes wide open and her jaw set. She wasn't talking, not because she had nothing to say, but because she couldn't. Finally, she relaxed her body.

"Boy!"

"Boy?"

"It's, uh, I'm. . . . I mean, I . . . I . . . (gulp of champagne), I don't know what to say."

"Well, if you could say, would it be positive or negative?" Always the insecure artist, our Leo.

Dara kept her head down and shook it slowly from side to side.

"They're dizzying, overwhelming, scary in how good they are. They're me. My innermost core, my bared and sometimes writhing soul. It's amazing that you can know me so well. It's spectacular genius that you can paint it this way. I'm literally breathless, flattered beyond words. You've made me feel like some sort of goddess. Like this is the temple of Athena– except it's Athena with a brain tumor. Even if you didn't know me, you'd know me. I feel flayed open and exposed as well as elated and proud." You don't keep Dara speechless for long.

"Someone else had better do the brochure design for this one."

"They're not going to be for sale. Not while I'm alive. They're too important to me Besides, they're my safety net in case."

"In case, what?"

"In case you ever get stupid again."

That morning was the first time we had really been alone together on our terms and undistracted. We sipped champagne and savored the moment. The moment was very nice. Dara broke the mood.

"There's more."

"Okay, tell me."

"No, I mean more paintings. There's something missing. What's missing?" She wasn't asking a question, she was demanding an answer.

"There are three more. The one on the easel, and two I haven't started yet. The one on the easel is when I asked you to go to Paris with me. The other two are you and Gwen as a child and you and Gwen right before she left to get married."

"You've left something out."

"What?"

"I don't know, but you're not showing me something."

"Why do you say that?"

"I don't know. I can just feel it. Am I right?"

"Maybe."

"Maybe? What does that mean, *maybe*?"

"There's another painting, but it's only for me. No one else will ever see it."

"What are you going to do, burn it on your death bed using your death throe to light the match?"

"Something like that."

"Is it of me?"

"Yes."

"Then why keep it from me? It's something I did or said or thought, so I've already experienced it. How bad can it be?"

"It's not bad at all. It's almost too good. You know how you said that these paintings bared your soul, and I said that my soul was in them too? Well, this painting is a lot more me than you. Almost pure lust and desire and need. You may think I'm too sick when you've seen it."

"Leo, if you haven't scared me off by now, this painting won't do it. At least I don't think so."

"Okay, but if you don't like it, I won't be able to destroy it while I'm alive. I promise no one else will ever see it."

"Did Ellen see it when you showed her the others?"

I chuckled.

"When you see it, you'll know the answer. Here's a hint: No."

"So, where is it?"

"Are you sure you want to see it?"

"I've never seen you like this before, Leo. You being shy about a painting of yours."

"It's not the painting. The painting is fine. Maybe even great. It's just that it's a paean to my sick, tortured mind, and you don't need to witness my depravity."

"I already know your sick, tortured mind and I love every Freudian synapse in it– now go get the painting."

I brought it out. Out to Dara. My heart beat faster even as I carried it to her. This was the first time I could look at the painting without sobbing, but the image on the canvas still beat me with its intensity. I should have known that it was okay to show it to Dara. Dara had loved every scribble I had ever scribbled, and this was a major work. A major work.

Dara started from the couch across the room and slowly approached the canvas. She spent what seemed like hours just staring at it. Her eyes were positively boiling over with first surprise, then amazement, then . . .

She turned to me as if to say something, but her face got closer and closer and her open mouth closed over mine. She ripped– ripped! with buttons flying– her blouse off and stepped out of her shorts. Before I could say anything, we were naked and rolling all over the studio floor in a surreal explosion of images as I held the naked real Dara tight to me and our rolling bodies crashed into and toppled all those pictures of Dara. Dara of all ages, and Dara of all moods, in our faces and under our bodies as we tried to avoid crushing them without ceding a calorie of our heat.

We had made love many times since Dara had returned, but always in that dreamy, melting, karma-rich interface of our two selves. There was nothing Zen about this– I couldn't have spelled *Zen* during the thick of it. We explored passions that went back to our first meeting, we went through pleasure and lust and a hyper-awareness of our bodies and our commingling electrons. We were both pure animal and intensely intellectual about what we were doing. We skipped dimensions and several times, I'm sure, defied the laws of physics.

Fueled by almost a year of separation and half a case of champagne– a sublime combination– we were in our bodies, feeling every nuance of physical sex, and outside of our bodies, proudly observing our performance. The dizzying moment went on and on and on, neither of us wanting it to end.

Then it did. We lay back in a heap, not daring to touch one another, too hot and too drained to move or think. The studio lay in shambles with paintings and easels and furniture all over the place, and we lay gasping for air as our bodies ran rivulets of sweat onto the floor.

"So Dara, did you like the painting?"

We laughed, which made breathing even more difficult, which made us laugh harder. Dara opened another bottle of champagne and poured half of it over our bodies, still laughing. We drank the other half straight from the bottle, in turns, whenever we could catch our breath long enough to take a gulp.

Half walking, half crawling, naked, wet and giving off wavy little smell lines of sex and sweat and champagne, we made our way to the shower. Though starting on opposite sides of the oversized shower stall, rinsing and soaping our own bodies back to reality, we kept getting closer and closer and found ourselves, still wet, having sex on a pile of bath towels on the bathroom floor– just as passionate, if considerably briefer, as the first time.

After it was over, we went to my bed where we barely had the energy to hug and kiss a few times before we fell asleep. I awoke about an hour later to Dara's caresses, and we made love one more time in a slower and much more loving, but equally passionate manner.

Dara had to return home to relieve the babysitter before we had the chance to talk about anything that we had done, or anything that had happened between us. She went home and I went to the studio to straighten up. Inexplicably, that one painting had somehow survived upright in the easel during all our thrashing about, almost as if that Dara were supervising the whole scene– sitting there, as I had placed it, high and aloof over the rubble and remnants of the passion it had inspired.

I lovingly put that painting away and straightened out the rest of the studio to be able to get to work immediately, the next time I came to the studio. After a last, silent good-bye to all the other Daras, I went home to the real one.

Chapter 30

The young babysitter sat in a straight-backed chair near the door, her clasped hands between her knees, her head bowed The air was foul and heavy, and the sound of Carrie's happy chatter rang hollow and incongruous in the twilight shadows. Gwen had slipped out of the house some time during the afternoon.

The teenager wasn't responsible for watching Gwen. There hadn't been any calls to the house, but she couldn't remember exactly when she'd last seen the missing woman. Even when Gwen was in a room with you, she blended in with the background, so it was easy not to notice her.

The police, unable to do anything for forty-eight hours, recommended that Dara call the airlines, bus and train stations. She paused just long enough to give me a quick rundown of the situation. The last time Gwen had run from Dara, she'd gone to the motel where she used to work, but when Dara called him, the owner didn't even know that Gwen was in town.

Gwen had taken all the money Dara kept on hand in a foyer drawer– for tips, deliveries and overdue mail– about forty or fifty dollars. That was probably all the money Gwen had with her. Marcus hadn't allowed her to have any credit cards, so wherever she was going, she'd have to go on limited funds. With that small amount of money, air travel wasn't likely, so we concentrated on trains and, especially, on buses.

Her destination was obvious. She'd go to Oregon to look for Marcus. Most people would consider their options and have a plan. Gwen would just go, in her fog, in her delusion, and in her need. She'd assume that if it was important enough to her, she would get there.

A bus would take Gwen the furthest for the money she had, and that's what a person with a plan would have chosen. With Gwen, there was no way of knowing what she had done. Because we weren't quite sure when she'd left (sometime between ten and four), she could be anywhere.. Nevertheless, I drove down the roads toward the expressway, and drove a few exits west to see if she was hitching, and still in the area.

Nothing worked. As time passed and Gwen hadn't called, and we'd run out of ideas, we just kept retrying the old ones.

Dara refused to be shaken by Gwen's disappearance, remaining focused and efficient throughout the evening. Her cool approach left nothing for me to do except make Dara coffee, keep Carrie busy, and try to think of new ideas. After a few hours of unproductive fretting, I had an inspiration.

We were focusing on the wrong end of the trip. No matter how she got to Oregon, she'd have to think of a way, with limited resources, to find Marcus once she got there. Linear thought was not her forte, so predicting her moves was mostly guesswork.

There were two people to whom she might turn to for help in Oregon. She must have called at least one of them. Alice was the more likely of the two, but beyond her first name and approximately where she lived, I knew nothing else about her. Although Gwen associated Marie with me, she might call her if she had no place else to turn.

Although Marie hadn't heard from Gwen, she was able, through determination and a lot of back and forth calling, to come up with Alice's phone number. Once Dara got past Alice's difficult husband, Alice was very helpful and understanding.

"She called me yesterday. I'll tell you what I told her– I haven't seen that bastard, Marcus, for months; he certainly hasn't been back to their trailer recently." Gwen had asked Alice to go into her trailer and get the phone number of Marcus' parents.

Dara reached Marcus' father on the first try.

"This is Dara Harrington, Gwen's mother, do you know who Gwen is?"

"Sure, Dara. We haven't met Gwen yet, but she called us this morning looking for Marcus. Carole and I thought they were out in Oregon and everything was fine. Do you know what's going on?" Dara gave Richard Davis a brief rundown of the recent events. His reaction was real, the shock and distress in his voice wasn't manufactured..

"I couldn't help her. We haven't heard from Marcus since they had the baby." He took Dara's number and promised to call if he had any news.

A good idea with initial promise, but we were right back to where we'd started. Gwen was still very weak and anemic, and her trip West would be a lot of strain on her. In addition, she had absolutely no experience with devising a plan of action and seeing it all the way through. One or both of us would have to go to Oregon and hope that she contacted either Alice or Marie so we could intercept her.

In the end, Dara went and I stayed behind. One of us had to stay at home in case Gwen called in. Dara went because there was no question in her mind that she would go.

That was fine with me. I was happy to have the old Dara back. What wasn't fine was that, just when Dara and I had gotten back together, Marcus, by way of Gwen, was, once again, splitting us asunder. When we kissed good-bye at the airport the next morning, we had no idea how long it would be until we saw each other again. Just when we thought that Marcus couldn't bother us any more, he was, from long distance and second hand, separating us one more time.

In a paranoid stream of consciousness sequence that came to me while driving back from the airport, I formulated a new Marcus theory. What if Gwen was not the real object of Marcus' sadistic evil? What if he was really out to get Dara? Or Dara and me? What could Dara or I have done to Marcus, whom we didn't know before he came into Gwen's life– and while I was on the subject, just exactly how did he come into Gwen's life?– that would make him hate us? If we were the objects of his loathing, he had successfully left his mark on us. What better way to destroy a parent than to systematically destroy her child and flaunt it in her face? Besides hurting us by abusing Gwen, Marcus had also driven a wedge between Dara and me, straining our relationship to its limits.

Was Marcus clever enough to have thought of all that? Was he evil enough to try it? If it were only that Marcus had nineteenth century views about marriage and women, and had no concept of how to treat a twenty-first century wife, his behavior would still have been unforgivable, but not as satanic as planning the destruction of Gwen in order to hurt Dara.

As much as I wanted to believe in my Marcus qua Sinister Plotter theory, I had met Marcus and found him to be a crazed macho psychotic– the Manson look– and little else. He hadn't demonstrated any imaginative skills, or any theatrical flair. The man was dull-normal, not clever, and he was far too rigid to deviate from established patterns of behavior. Wife beaters were intellectually little men with grandiose ideas. Still, I clung to my theory because, in a perverse way, it comforted me.

Back home, I dismissed the babysitter. Playing with Carrie was a welcome distraction, especially since there was nothing for me to do but wait for the phone to ring.

Dara called at eight the next morning to give me her phone number. She had nothing to report except that she was driving out to see Alice that day. With no money and no other place to go, Gwen would have to go to her trailer. Dara suggested that she might just as well move into Gwen's trailer and wait for her there, but I told her not to make any plans until she'd seen it.

She called me back a few hours later. Gwen hadn't contacted Alice again, and there were no clues to Marcus' whereabouts in the trailer– which Dara had, as I expected, found appalling. My East Village neighborhood was a well-manicured suburb in comparison. Dara gave Alice a hundred dollars and promised her more if she called the minute Gwen showed up. Other than dinner with Marie that night, she had no other plans except to wait.

"Call a private detective. Someone who knows what he's doing could track down both of them. There's enough information to get a start."

"How do I know whom to call?"

"I don't know. Maybe the police can help."

"Like they did in Forest Hills?"

"Then the Yellow Pages, or the lawyer who helped me with Carrie. Try the police first. We haven't broken any laws yet, this time."

"Do you think a detective can really help?"

"This is what they do. Besides, it's the only idea I've come up with."

"Okay, what do we have to lose? I'm going to say good-bye and start making some phone calls."

After that, it was a matter of waiting; Dara in Oregon and me in Northport. I had the better deal since I had Carrie to keep me occupied. With Marie back at her job, Dara was alone. She called me four or five times a day out of boredom and frustration.

Chapter 31

Walking the two miles from Dara's house to avoid the expense of a taxi, Gwen had thirty-seven dollars and some change when she got to the bus station. No one had stopped to give her a ride, so she had spent all her energy before her cross-country trip even began.

Her money would get her to western Pennsylvania. Then, she'd have to go the rest of the way on foot– hitching and hoping for the largesse of a long-haul trucker. After paying for her ticket, there was less than two dollars left. Two dollars for food and whatever else she might need on her way. She'd have to find Marcus immediately, and beg him to take her back.

There was always, no matter how much she didn't want to acknowledge it, the safety net of Dara and me. We were an escape she was unprepared to take. Gwen hated us because Dara made it clear that her help came with a price tag that she couldn't stomach. Rather than be thankful to us for rescuing her, she blamed us, and especially Dara, for taking her away from Marcus, and for being apart from him.

Gwen had hated herself throughout her life; a hate she hadn't even shared with Dr. Jamison. She was smart enough to fool everyone– Dara, Dr. Jamison, her teachers, and from time to time, herself. Once, there had only been Dara and Gwen. Dara wasn't enough. Sometimes, she was too much.

As a mother, Dara was often overbearing. Although she was never like that with me, she was often like that at work, intimidating many of the people who worked for her. They forgave her, at least partially, because she knew what she was doing and the finished product was always successful. There was, however, no one at work who considered Dara a friend –except, of course, Marty, and we all know how that turned out.

Somehow, in his sadistic, cruel and degrading way, Marcus had gotten in the way of Gwen's self-hatred, almost as if his degradation of Gwen made it unnecessary for Gwen to do the same thing to herself. She mistook that for love, then mistook the absence of self-loathing as a sign of her increased happiness when she was with Marcus.

Dara had loved Gwen too much. Marcus had abused Gwen too much. Yet Marcus was the one whom she loved, and Dara whom she hated. The fatherless Gwen yearned for a dominant male figure to both guide her and subdue Dara. I didn't count– I had my own issues: painting, the fugues– at least not in any way that mattered. My role was to balance, not prevent.

Gwen embraced Marcus' domination as a sign that he cared enough to pay attention to her, a sign that he loved her. Once in Marcus' world, there was no going back for Gwen. She had tried Dara's way, even had come back to Dara's house. She'd had enough, and she was going back to Marcus. Gwen wasn't going to live the hypocrisy of Dara's home where Dara had made her give up Marcus, and Dara had made her give up Carrie. She would have to deal with getting Carrie back later, when she had Marcus's help. Reclaiming Marcus, though, was something she must do on her own. Gwen would show Marcus *and* Dara that she could do it– Marcus would be proud of her.

Using her last reserves of will, Gwen had been standing on the shoulder of the Interstate for about an hour, unable to get a trucker to stop. A police officer in a cruiser ordered Gwen off the road.

"It's a hazard to be here, ma'am, you could get killed."

"I need to get to Oregon. My husband's sick and I have to see him."

"I'm sorry, ma'am. You can't stay here."

Gwen walked away from the patrol car. She walked off down the road, intending to ignore the policeman, and resume hitching as soon as he drove away. The officer was persistent, and when he asked Gwen for an I.D., she panicked. Dara may have already notified the authorities to be on the lookout for her. She might be arrested for vagrancy when the policeman discovered that she had no money. The weak and scared young woman left the road and sat in the bushes behind a gas station for an hour before resuming her post.

A car stopped for her. Though she had hoped for a trucker who would give her a long ride, she needed to get out of the area and was grateful for any offer. The driver was a middle-aged traveling salesman, weary and resigned, though pleasant enough. He shared some snacks that he had with Gwen. Unfortunately, he wasn't going far.

Just after midnight, the salesman pulled into the parking lot of a motel. He planned to sleep in the back seat of the car, and told his passenger that she could stay in the front if she liked. Gwen accepted.

In the morning, she accompanied her new friend to a donut shop and used most of her remaining money to buy a bagel. The salesman didn't finish his third cup of coffee, so Gwen drank what was left. The man drove Gwen to the Interstate, wished her well, and left.

Gwen ran into some luck when she was, almost immediately, picked up by a truck heading west to Nebraska. There was a team of drivers, and Gwen had to stay on the mattress they kept behind the front seat. The men were self-conscious at first about their language, apologizing to *the lady* after almost every sentence. Gwen fell asleep.

The drivers drove right on through, stopping occasionally for food and coffee. Every time they stopped, they roused Gwen to ask if she wanted to eat. Except for once, when she got out to use the toilet, she slept. The drivers never realized that she didn't eat because she had no money. They left Gwen at the roadside on the far side of Lincoln, just before dawn.

There was very little traffic at that time of day. Gwen was chilly from the damp of the early morning fog. She hadn't bathed or changed clothes in days, had slept in cars and in trucks and hadn't eaten much since leaving Northport. Weak, so weak from anemia, her injured ribs and jaw throbbed constantly in the damp weather compounding her misery. Her cross country trek– which still had a long way to go– had taken more resolve than anything she'd ever done.

Her overpowering need to find Marcus was the only reason she was able to go on at all. The quest for Marcus was so important because it demonstrated her fidelity and love. The trek would address Marcus' deepest insecurity– show him that Gwen would give up Dara and me for him.

Gwen felt so lost, spiritually lost. Her internal resources were as used up as her money, and she was uncertain that she could complete her journey. Not just the physical journey to Oregon, but the symbolic journey from child to adult, from girl to woman, a journey away from her mother's control, and a reaffirmation of her love for Marcus. Failing to complete her quest meant failure in her life.

Back at the very beginning, as she walked wearily down the road to the bus station in Northport, Gwen had shifted a single quarter to another pocket in her jeans. In case. The quarter was an admission of defeat, the money for *the phone call*, the phone call to ask us to take her back. Back to Dara. Back to me. Back to hell.

In a relatively dry place in the bushes along the side of the road, Gwen slept until the sounds of early morning rush-hour traffic woke her.

No one was willing to stop for her up until the traffic lightened, a few hours later. Had she even thought about the perils of a young woman hitching alone in the middle of nowhere, she still, out of desperation, would have accepted a ride from anyone. Gwen never considered her safety.

The driver seemed benign enough. He was smiley and very polite, and spoke with a slight Southern drawl. The man was young and might have been handsome under his unshaven growth and his dirty long hair. Gwen noticed the smell of whiskey on his breath, so wasn't surprised when he pulled a flask from his shirt pocket and offered her a drink.

She accepted. Not that she wanted alcohol, but because she was cold from the morning spent alongside the road, and she was hungry. Very hungry. The driver was going all the way to Washington State, so she ignored her apprehensions about driving in a huge semi with a drunk trucker. Gwen was determined to put up with whatever was necessary, and pray for no accidents.

"It's about time you thanked me for picking you up."

"I'm sorry, I thought I did. Thanks again."

"I don't mean like that. Come over and sit next to me." The trucker patted the seat by his side. His manner and his speech changed . He gave her specific orders with graphic vulgarity. Gwen stayed where she was, concentrating on her goal. If this lewd, drunk idiot was her way to Marcus, a little dirty talk didn't matter. But the trucker kept on drinking and the tone of his sexual demands became more threatening. He alternated between rubbing his own crotch and grabbing for Gwen's thigh, which was just beyond his reach. Or mostly.

When he unzipped his fly, Gwen asked the driver to let her out. He pulled over into the break down lane, and Gwen thought he would let her go. As she started to open the door, the heavy-breathing bastard grabbed her arms and pinned them behind her. With his free hand, he pawed the front of Gwen's jeans and she realized he was going to rape her.

What he was doing, however, was looking for money in her pockets. All that he found was some change. Frustrated, the enraged man drew Gwen close and kissed her. She bit his lip and struggled out of his grasp. Gwen pulled the door latch, and tried to jump out of the cab, but the trucker had thrown the truck into gear and was already moving onto the highway, gaining speed.

Fearing for her life, now, Gwen clung to the dashboard and tried to get hold of the open door that was swinging wildly as the truck lurched back onto the road. The driver turned and shoved Gwen out of the open cab with his foot. She landed hard and rolled into the shoulder.

Chapter 32

The detective found Gwen in Nebraska four days after Dara hired him. A female trucker named Karen Jenkins had spotted Gwen's body along the interstate roadside and had stopped to check. Gwen was alive, but disoriented and unable to provide a coherent story. When the police arrived and found her covered with dirt and dried blood, they took her to a local hospital for care. Gwen had refused to provide any information about herself until the detective, having canvassed all the police stations and hospitals from Northport to Oregon, gave them her name. Confronted with that information, she admitted who she was.

Dara went to Nebraska.

I'm a rich man. A very rich man. I don't live like a rich man because my obsession is painting, an occupation made up of mostly poor men and women hoping to become rich. Even though it doesn't cost a lot to be a painter, I provided myself with a state of the art studio in a beautiful location, and I deprive myself of nothing.

By comparison to me, Dara is not a rich woman. By comparison to most other people, she is. She holds a prestigious position at a major New York advertising agency with a commensurate salary. It doesn't matter anyway because what is mine is Dara's and vice versa. My point is that either one of us could afford to fly back and forth from coast to coast, stay in hotels, rent cars, hire detectives, pay for information and whatever else it would take to find Gwen. Parents with fewer resources would probably lose their children under similar circumstances.

I wasn't sure that we hadn't, anyway.

The reunion between mother and daughter in Gwen's hospital room couldn't have been, and wasn't, comfortable for either of them. They had played out the same scene once before, although this time, Gwen was more aware of Dara's arrival. And more demoralized. There was no escape from Dara and Dara's judgmental motherliness. Severing Dara's stifling bonds wasn't to be; not yet, anyway. Gwen was in the middle of nowhere, penniless and out of choices, and needed to drink from Dara's well one more time. She would drink, but she didn't have to like it.

From the time she had gotten off the bus in Pennsylvania. until she was admitted to the hospital, Gwen hadn't eaten much of anything Her run-in with the truck driver had left her bruised, but without any serious injuries. The police had taken her to the hospital because there had been no place else to keep her– it was the hospital or jail– and the captain, who had a teenage daughter of his own, was reluctant to put her in a jail cell after her bad road experience. Instead, he appealed to the local hospital to care for her pending identification.

Keeping Gwen in a hospital room instead of jail was something that could be done in a small town that never would have been possible in a large city. Gwen was uncooperative at first. She understood her predicament, but was putting off the inevitability of having to call us for help. She refused to eat until the doctor threatened her with tube feedings.

As long as Gwen continued to eat, there was no reason for her to remain hospitalized. In fact, now that Gwen had been identified and a relative had shown up to claim her, they wouldn't be able to keep her any longer.

Gwen was sullen and avoided Dara's gaze, refusing to talk about what she'd done and why she had run away.

"You've got two options. Either we can talk things out and come to an agreement about what to do next, or I'm going home and you can handle this on your own."

"Just get me out of here, and we'll talk for however long you want."

"It doesn't work that way. I don't do another thing for you until we've talked."

"You're always trying to control me. All you ever think about is yourself and whether you're getting what *you* want. You pretend you're this great understanding and giving mother, but you never consider my needs. Right or wrong doesn't matter as long as you get your way. That's what Marcus says about you."

"My first condition is that you never quote Marcus to me again."

Silence. Hate-filled silence. Turning the face away silence. Body language silence.

"Here's the number where I'm staying. I'll be there until I can get a flight home tomorrow. Call me if you want to talk."

Dara handed Gwen a matchbook from her motel and turned to leave. Capitulation was the young woman's only choice. In words, anyway.

"Mom, don't go. I'll talk to you. I have to."

"Don't lay that on me. You have choices, and you know what they are. I may be your only rational choice, but that's just my opinion.

You make the decision. Whatever it is, though, you're going to have to live with it this time. Neither Leo nor I are going to come riding in on a white horse any more."

"Sit down . . . please."

"This is the situation as I see it. However much you love Marcus, whatever you think of him, he has abused you mentally and physically from the moment you got married. He almost beat you to death, and he killed your unborn baby. Then he abandoned you at the emergency room and has made no attempt to find out if you're still alive, or what has become of you or Carrie. Stop me if I'm wrong."

"You just don't understand Marcus. I know all that sounds bad, but not if you really knew Marcus."

"I'm getting to that. You, on the other hand, were brought up in a home where, no matter what other failings we had as parents, Leo and I always treated each other with love, respect and trust. You allowed yourself to be denigrated and enslaved by Marcus. You rejected and renounced Leo who has been more of a father to you than most people's real fathers are, and who, nevertheless, rushed to your rescue when he got the call. You ran from my home, without word, like you were some kind of prisoner, and you've all but ignored your infant daughter who needs her mother. And the only explanation you can give, the only explanation you have ever given is, *You don't understand Marcus.* You said it when you eloped, you said it to us when we came to see you in Forest Hills, and you said it to Leo the other night.

"It's time to make us understand Marcus. It's time to explain why his behavior is okay, why you not only tolerate it, but go back begging for more. No. No. That's not right. You don't have to make me understand, you don't have to explain it to me. You have to explain it to yourself. What you're doing is irrational and self-destructive. Explain that to yourself. And while you're at it, okay, tell me too, so I can explain to Carrie why her mother ran off to get herself killed."

Dara was determined not to shout, but by the end of her tirade, her eyes were molten and she was positively hissing. No wonder Gwen averted her gaze.

These were exactly the recriminations from which Gwen had run. She didn't like being made to feel that she had failed herself, or that her marriage to Marcus was a mistake. Nor could she bear to hear us talk about Marcus like he was a monster.

"Marcus loves me!"

"Then where is he?"

"You don't und. . . ." She stopped herself. "I mean, Marcus has suffered a lot, too. His mother ignored him when he was a child, and his father was too weak to do anything about it. She ruled the house. He was determined not to be a weak man like his father. He believes in real men and real women who know their roles and keep to them.

"When he was in college, all he ever met were "liberated" women who sickened him with their airs and their licentiousness. Then, when he went to work, nobody understood how smart he was. They didn't appreciate him and passed him over for their sons-in-law and nephews who weren't nearly as competent as Marcus. So he ended up with a nowhere position in the company, a job he did and did well without complaining.

"As soon as he tried to show some initiative, they fired him– said he was misrepresenting the company. And all the time he was going through that, he had to deal with you and Leo who just assumed he was bad and never gave him a chance. In all his life he was ridiculed and demeaned. He was never taken seriously by anyone, not his parents, not his teachers, not his peers and not his bosses. Okay, so now do you understand?"

"What you're saying is that everyone is out to get Marcus?"

"You're twisting my words like you always do. You refuse to listen. That's why I've never tried to explain before."

"Am I twisting your words? Which ones am I twisting? The ones where you said his mother ignored him, his father was too weak to support him, the girls at college were snobby dirt-balls? Or the ones about not being appreciated at work and being fired for trying to sell securities when he was unlicenced to do so, and was supposed to be scouting strip malls?"

"It's not like that. If only you knew him."

"I don't know him because he has refused to meet me. What's that all about?"

"He doesn't approve of you." She said this in a barely audible mumble with her head down and turned away.

"And you're okay with that?"

"I don't agree with him, but I see why he thinks it. Marcus has very strong moral values. He doesn't believe in casual sex or divorce. So when he sees you living with a divorced man, he considers it fornication and adultery. You've got to admit that's what it is."

"So, what you're saying is that my fifteen-year relationship with a man like Leo Schultz is immoral and wrong, but wife beating and abuse are somehow moral and okay?"

"When you put it like that, no. It's true Marcus has a bad temper and sometimes gets carried away, but he really does care for me."

"Then why haven't you heard from him?"

"I think he's afraid. Of you. And the police. That's why I have to get to him so I can help him. I can straighten everything out. At least with the police."

"Gwen, don't you understand that it's never okay to beat your wife? I don't care how stressed out you are, how many people are after you, how bad the situation is. IT'S NEVER OKAY!"

Gwen bent her head and sat silently. Tears started to flow copiously down her cheeks. When she spoke, her voice was barely audible. When she spoke, it was the voice of a broken little girl.

"Sometimes I deserve it."

Dara took Gwen in her arms, clutching Gwen's head to her breast in the pose that has symbolized maternal love and caring since long before the Madonna. She hugged Gwen hard and stroked her hair. Tears slid from her own eyelids.

"Gwen, my Gwen. You're so beautiful, so kind, so good. What could you ever possibly have done to deserve to be beaten?"

"I need Marcus. Our good times together are the only thing I've ever done well. I try hard to keep him loving me, but I can't always be how Marcus wants me to be. When he punishes me, he's not being mean, it's his way to remind me how good it can be and what I need to do to make it stay good. How else would I know how to please him?"

Dara was done. She had forced the showdown, made Gwen talk to her, controlled Gwen— not unlike the way Marcus had controlled her, too. And she had gotten nowhere. She had upset herself and Gwen. And she had gotten nowhere. There was nothing else to do, no potions, no prayers, no tricks to make it all better. Not even any words left to say.

"If finding Marcus is what you're determined to do, I can't stop you. You'd only run away again. So here's my offer. I'll go back to Oregon with you and help you find Marcus. Once I've met him, and I will meet him this time, you're on your own if you decide to stay with him. Also, I'm going to put a thousand dollars in an emergency bank account for you. If you need the money, it's yours. If you decide to give it to Marcus, that's your decision. There won't be any more, either from me or Leo. After that, we'll always be your parents and we'll always love you but, otherwise, Leo and I are going to get on with our lives."

"You'll really help me find Marcus?" That was the only thing she had heard.

"If that's what you want, yes. And one more thing. Leo and I are going to take care of Carrie. Don't you or Marcus even think about getting her from us. As you keep reminding me, you're a grown woman and you are entitled to make decisions about your own life, but I won't have you endangering an innocent child. Just so you know. Now get your clothes on, and let's get you out of here."

We spent three hours on the phone that night. First, Dara gave me a detailed report of everything that had happened, and about her conversation with Gwen. Then, I commiserated with Dara as she metaphorically gnashed her teeth and rent her clothes. I gave Dara a report on Carrie who had begun saying *da da* which, I insisted, was Carrie-ese for *Dara*.

Dara and Gwen flew back to Oregon the next morning, and asked the detective to find Marcus. The only lead to Marcus was his girlfriend. Gwen had found Marcus at the girlfriend's apartment when she had run away from me the first time, so she knew where she lived. The now ex-girlfriend hadn't seen Marcus in six weeks, and didn't know what had become of him– not since he had attempted to start controlling her life.

Marcus had no credit cards, no bank accounts, and no friends, all of which secured the impenetrability of his disappearance. The trail was stone cold. The detective wasn't optimistic.

"Well, Gwen, this is where I get off. You're welcome to come back with me."

"Can't we stay around a little longer? In case he comes back?"

"I'm going home as soon as I can get a flight. You're on your own."

"What am I going to do?"

"I don't know. Here's the money I was going to put into an account for you. The emergency appears to be here now. It'll last you a while. If you decide to come home, I'll get you a ticket, but that's all I'm going to do. I'll always be your mother, and I love you very much, but since there's no way to stop you, it's time to say good-bye. If you think I'm turning my back on you, it's not because I'm abandoning you, it's only that I can't bear to watch you do this to yourself. I hope you get what you're after."

They embraced and kissed. Dara got into her rental car, not daring to look back. She was leaving her daughter, her only child, in a dilapidated, filthy trailer in a seedy trailer park, longing for her abusive, deranged husband, and willing to do anything to get him back. Dara was bereft, but determined.

At the airport the next day, she still had that resolute, if troubled, look on her face. When she vented her rage and her frustration and her impotence to me in an agitated but animated way, I knew she was going to be okay.

That left only Gwen.

Chapter 33

Totally devastated, Gwen called us about three weeks later. She was being evicted from her trailer for nonpayment of four months back rent. The money Dara had left her was not enough to pay the back rent and stay on. There had been no word from or about Marcus, and with no alternatives, she was coming back to Carrie.

We had mixed emotions about her return. We much preferred that Gwen be safe with us than anywhere else. On the other hand, we were a happy little family— Dara, Carrie and I— and Dara and I were together, at last, the way we always should have been. When it came down to it, though, of course we wanted her with us.

Gwen returned against her will, and broken. She had gone from the security of our household to the isolation of her life with Marcus without ever having to confront the real world. Although she had maintained her job at the motel while she lived with us, it was only to avoid Dara's censure. Her lack of experience ill-prepared her for coping on her own. It never occurred to Gwen to get a job and find a place to live and stay on her own while she waited for the illusive Marcus.

Living together wasn't going to be easy for us or Gwen. She'd resent us for reminding her— whether in actual words or merely by being around her– of what we thought about Marcus. In her mind, she was with us against her will. Our lives would be assaulted by a sullen and grieving Gwen, whose grief for her absent, wife-beating husband would tear at Dara's heart. Gwen's listlessness and the sadness of her indifference towards Carrie would permeate every aspect of our lives.

"One condition."

"What now?"

"You won't be a prisoner here. If you want to leave, tell us you're going. That's all."

"What else?"

"Nothing else. There'll be a ticket waiting for you at the counter whenever you get there. Let us know when you're coming, and we'll pick you up."

We tried to make the transition unthreatening for her. To her credit, she tried, too, acting less reclusive than the last time.

Judging from my experience with Carrie, missing out on Gwen's early years was a loss. The excitement of watching her change almost every day amazed me. Now, whenever either Dara or I came into the room, Carrie greeted us by name, calling each of us, *da da* in an excited and welcoming voice. What a shame if Gwen never allowed herself the opportunity to share her daughter's firsts. Carrie was also Gwen's only link with Marcus.

With Gwen's promise not to leave without telling us, Dara and I could go back to work. After a few unsuccessful attempts at leaving mother and daughter alone together, we had to keep the baby sitters during the day while Gwen was there, as ridiculous as that sounds. Dara asked Gwen about her emotional estrangement from Carrie.

"You and Leo have taken her away from me. You told me so."

"I told you that I wouldn't let you take her back to Marcus. You're still her mother. Why don't you act like one?"

"You mean act more like *my* perfect mother?"

"I never ignored you, Gwen."

"No, you were too busy bossing me around. The imperious Dara Harrington. No mere mortal, especially a kid, could avoid doing Dara Harrington's bidding. No questions asked."

"I'm sorry you hate me. I thought I was carrying off the single mother thing quite well. That's even more reason why you shouldn't want Carrie to hate you. Don't copy my mistakes."

"If Carrie and me get dependent on each other, what's she going to do when I go back to Marcus?"

"How will you find him?"

"He'll find me. I expect him to call soon. He loves me."

"What if he doesn't? Then what will you do?"

"He will. He has to."

Weeks passed and there was no word from Marcus. Dara was working full-time now, and putting in a lot of overtime as well. Her enthusiasm about returning to work led her to take on more projects than she realistically could handle, but she was totally engrossed and became more and more relaxed the harder she worked.

I was working long hours in my studio finishing the last three paintings in the Dara cycle. The paintings would never be shown in my lifetime, so I wanted to write something about them in order to explain them, and myself. I was a painter, not a writer, and had trouble writing about the paintings– it was much harder than I anticipated, and took more time than I thought.

With the approach of winter and its shortened days, Gwen's demeanor grew as dark as the night skies. By November, she had been living with us for four months with no word from Marcus. The trailer in Oregon had long since been repossessed, and Alice and her husband had moved to Colorado, so Gwen's last links to Marcus were coming undone. She did nothing all day except wait for the phone to ring.

Urging Gwen to get involved in something– our perennial cry of *do something*– was always met with hostility, regressing to name calling and anger on both sides. The pre-Marcus Gwen did nothing, but was content, if not happy. The present Gwen was miserable. How much longer could the situation go on?

"What am I going to tell Carrie when she asks me who that stranger is who lived with us when she was growing up?" Dara's favorite approach.

"You'll probably be dead when she grows up. You won't have to tell her anything." Gwen's expression was venomous, her hate evident. Dara's death couldn't come soon enough.

"Cute. What I'm trying to say, in my overbearing but loveable way, is, why don't you get involved with Carrie? Marcus isn't coming back for you. The one nice thing that can be said about your marriage is that it produced Carrie. Why don't you hold on to that? Someday, when you get hold of yourself, you may want to live alone with Carrie or maybe even, and I know I'm treading on dangerous ground here, find another man whom you love and want to live with."

"I'm married. That would be adultery. Is that what you want me to do in front of Carrie? In case you haven't noticed, and despite what you want, I have a husband. He's the one I want. The only one I want. The only one that matters."

"Despite what Marcus says, divorce is not a contract with evil and divorced women are not whores."

"I haven't given up on Marcus yet. If he hasn't called me, it must be that he can't. I know he will as soon as he can."

"Why beat yourself . . . sorry, bad choice of words when talking about Marcus. Why not let yourself be Gwen, and just enjoy life for a change? That's all I want for you."

"I'm nothing without Marcus. How can I enjoy anything when I'm not with him? Marcus is my joy. He is my man. When you meet Marcus, you'll see what I mean when I say that he's special. Marcus demands excellence from his wife, and I'm trying to learn how to be excellent for him. Sometimes I disappoint him. Sometimes he gets frustrated with me, but it doesn't mean he doesn't love me. If his temper is the price I have to pay to be with him, it's well worth it."

"He almost killed you!"

"It wasn't as bad as you make it sound. Anyway, it was an accident."

"Leo has met Marcus several times. He doesn't think he's *special* at all."

"I wouldn't expect Leo to like Marcus. Men don't. Other men can't compete with Marcus. They're all too jealous and intimidated to try."

"Leo? Intimidated by Marcus? Why?"

"I've told you, Marcus is special."

"Yes, you've been telling us that Marcus is special since you met him, and yet you've never been able to say what makes him so special. You made an attempt, back in Nebraska– but, what exactly is it?

"Is it because he abuses you, or because he has outmoded views about women and marriage? Or is it his cowardice in refusing to meet me or Leo before you got married? Or maybe his trouble at work? There are lots of men who are out of work, abusive macho throwbacks. There's nothing *special* in any of that. So tell me, Gwen, where's the *special* part?"

Dara stopped Gwen's explanation of Marcus' world view, asking her to wait until I could hear it too. By the time Carrie was in bed that night, Gwen was eager to talk. The story she told wasn't her own interpretation of the man named Marcus Davis, it was a recitation of a manifesto.

"Marcus' thinking is years ahead of everyone else. It's a tribute to Marcus' genius that he didn't, like so many liberal assholes, discard old values out of hand. Instead, he embraced the patriarchal family, integrity and honesty as the cornerstone of his plan to *fix what's wrong with this country.*

"Because he's so progressive, he's misunderstood and not taken seriously. Even as a child, he was alienated by his views. His mother was little more than a slut who flitted from man to man as the winds blew her and her fortune beckoned. She hid behind feminism to cover her depravity, and laughed out loud at Marcus' beliefs. She had already violated every principle that Marcus held dear. Who was she to dismiss him?

"His father could successfully run a business, but couldn't control his wife's profligate spending and her haughtiness about her lifestyle and past. He couldn't stand up to his wife or hold her accountable for anything– *he never established the reign of his manhood in his own* home." Gwen actually used those words which, no doubt, came directly from Marcus.

"Marcus is sensitive, perhaps too sensitive for our present world. He remained alienated from his classmates and ridiculed for being different. They called him *crazy* and *loser* because he dared to be different. For instance, he refused to lower his moral standards to that of other teenage boys and girls. The high school and college girls avoided him because he confronted them with their harlotry; the boys avoided him because he scared away the girls. Teachers were always on his back to get counseling even though, publicly, they lauded free thinking and individuality.

"He ran into the same problems at work and preferred solitary positions where his talents would shine. But despite his impressive performance and obvious abilities, he was held back or fired by jealous superiors and peers.

"Marcus' vision is a world of isolated homesteads, like in frontier days, with a single dominant male head and a woman to tend his needs– efficiently, willingly and unquestioningly. A virgin bride who used her womanliness only for the pleasure of her husband and not for any of those half-baked liberal feminist causes." Marcus was looking for Mother Teresa in a camisole? How pathetic.

"If the single family, male-run household were the basic unit of our society, there would be no crime, no dissatisfaction, no greed and no animosity– not between races or sexes or classes. If a child misbehaved, his father would discipline him. If there were property disputes, men would fight over them in the time-honored ways of men. Everyone would know his or her place and what was expected of them. This is Marcus' genius and his contribution. His perseverance in his beliefs, despite ridicule and abuse, is his *specialness*.

Dara and I kept looking at each other during the early part of this dissertation, doing the eye equivalent of circling our temples with our forefingers, but we quickly realized it was counterproductive and stopped looking at each other at all. To our credit, neither of us laughed even once.

Gwen's humorless fervor was scary. How could you respond to someone who took Marcus' ranting seriously? I didn't have a clue. Dara evidently thought she should try.

"I still don't understand, Gwen. How do you go from everyone living in peace and harmony to beating your wife and abandoning your baby daughter?"

"That's all you focus on. That one thing. I keep telling you that Marcus isn't like that at all. He's just a perfectionist. Everyone has to sacrifice."

"What is Marcus sacrificing?"

"Look at all the so-called heroes of our time. Gandhi abandoned his family. Martin Luther King cheated on his wife whenever he could. So did JFK. Look at Nelson Mandela."

Dara and I both sighed. I controlled the volume of my sigh a little better than she did. What could we say? What was there left to say? Especially since Gwen didn't want to hear it.

"So, what are you hoping for? What do you want?"

"Just for Marcus to come get me."

"And then what?"

"Whatever Marcus wants. Whatever he tells me."

Chapter 34

What reason couldn't accomplish, time slowly did. More time passed, much more time, and still there was no word from Marcus. After so much time, Gwen could no longer fool herself into expecting his call. Disillusionment, and the anger generated by her frustration started to break through the shell of Gwen's depression. Lack of self-esteem was Gwen's problem, never stupidity. Time proved that Marcus wasn't going to live up to his self-proclaimed myth.

Slowly, Gwen shed layers of Marcus' influence, had less faith in his dogma, questioned everything about Marcus and her relationship with him. She no longer quoted him. By spring, her re-emergence became an almost visible event. As layers of clothes started to disappear, Gwen became less and less Marcus' wife and thrall, and more and more like something else. Not that she was back to being our daughter– no one wanted that. If anything, she was becoming a new Gwen, a different Gwen. An adult woman.

Her basic personality hadn't changed in any way. She remained apathetic and without goals or interests. But instead of waiting by the phone all day, she spent a little time with Carrie. Even though Carrie was now calling Gwen *mamamama* (and Dara *Dah* and me *Lo*), we still needed the baby sitters.

And, then, she began to read.

No longer just disinterestedly leafing through magazines, she was reading whole books from beginning to end. She set aside time to read, looked forward to reading. At first, she read slowly, taking several weeks to get through the first book. Then the switch got turned on– Gwen read voraciously and all the time.

Gwen had stopped reading when Marcus cut her off from the library and from the books Alice brought her. Soon after she started to read again, she began reading in great, hungry gulps of words: novels, history, feminist writing. Often, there were two or three books scattered around the house, which Gwen was reading simultaneously.

A common scene in the Harrington household was an evening on Dara's screened-in porch. All three of us would be reading, with either Dara or me reading to Carrie. So I guess all four of us were reading.

The life-commanding stimulus that we had hoped for when Gwen was twelve, expected when she had graduated from high school, and despaired over when she was twenty-four had, at last, happened. Gwen was interested in something. Reading.

She read.

Finishing most of the books on Dara's shelves, she bought new books for herself, gravitating toward women authors and feminist writing. The more she read other women's stories and personal accounts, the more she understood and could verbalize her own history. She talked about Marcus in a way that, only a few months before, she never would have tolerated. To our surprise and delight, she talked about Marcus in the past tense.

Perhaps Gwen's time with Marcus, however painful and abasing, had been necessary to get her from where she wasn't (anywhere) to where she was going. Though no one would have chosen such a physically and emotionally violent experience, it was Gwen's experience, and it had awakened her from her lethargy and had pointed her . . . where?

She kept on reading.

Gwen evolved, from an empty-headed lump to a neo-feminist, polemic spouting, jargon spewing, repetitive, unoriginal boor, and then to a thoughtful, reasoning young woman in search of herself. And she did it all in a matter of a few months. As she learned where she wanted to be, and where she had erroneously let herself be led, she developed a true sense of who she actually was. Gwen embraced her position as the middle point of the matriarchal Dara-Gwen-Carrie continuum by actively becoming a mother and reveling in the nascent friendship that was developing between her and Dara to replace the conflict-plagued mother-daughter relationship that had always existed.

Dara did her part too. Working long and hard at her job, she was too busy to waste time on meddling, so she seldom pushed Gwen, letting her change at her own pace. Dara remained positive, offered her opinion when asked, but otherwise let Gwen do her own decision making. The relief of witnessing a happier and, at last, involved Gwen allowed Dara and me to get back to the *us* that had been ignored and assaulted for so long.

Professionally, it was a very satisfying time for me, as well. I had completed the Dara cycle and was pleased with the end result. The *Daras*, or more accurately, my state of mind as I painted them, inspired a new cycle of paintings. Each of the new paintings represented a different emotion. Each emotion demanded its own style and substance– subject matter, use of color, shadowing, etc.

They were a lot of fun to do, but also draining because, while painting each emotion, I couldn't help but be in its perpetual state.

My home life was happy too. I was a privileged observer in a seraglio of three, each in her own manner, attractive women. Dara unfolded into her life and found satisfaction in all aspects of it. Carrie was learning to use the intricacies of her body and mind to make herself into a real human being. Gwen was learning the secret of focusing her potential towards an end. I just sat back and watched all this evolve and smiled an inward, beatific smile.

The next step in Gwen's transformation was her desire to do something active. She had already begun to take a more active role with Carrie who loved the extra attention. The baby sitters were becoming increasingly superfluous, and Gwen had to decide whether to eliminate them entirely, or find an interest outside the house. She did two things.

Gwen volunteered at a shelter for battered and abused women. She was a natural because she identified with the new women in the shelter who weren't yet ready to admit their reality to themselves. She also shared thoughts she'd culled from her extensive reading with some advanced groups of women who were further along in the healing process. The group participation helped Gwen understand her own problems, and her contribution reduced her own feelings of self-loathing.

And, she decided to formally divorce Marcus.

Gwen had neither seen nor heard from Marcus in more than eighteen months, and didn't expect or want to ever see him again. She felt a formal divorce would be both a final repudiation of the entire Marcus experience, and the impetus to make plans for her future.

Proving abuse would be easy– the hospital records alone were proof enough. There was also the testimony from Marie and Steve– in addition to my own– that they had heard Marcus verbally abuse and threaten Gwen and had seen the bruises on her body. Alice had witnessed or heard many beatings at the trailer park and couldn't wait to say so in court. The hard part was finding Marcus. The courts had to give him a chance to tell his side, and the process could be drawn out if he stayed underground.

I was the only one who was still afraid that Marcus would show up and make trouble. Dara never mentioned him anymore and Gwen now viewed him as the pathetic bully that he was. Although happy that she was no longer terrified of Marcus, I wasn't as confident as the others that the danger was over. I would have been relieved, for instance, if I had heard that Marcus had joined the French Foreign Legion or had become a monk in Tibet.

As I said, Dara didn't want to think about Marcus at all. Gwen and I discussed him at length, almost obsessively– the way Dara and I used to discuss Gwen– trying to figure out what had motivated him to be the way he was and why he'd focused his evil on Gwen.

Marcus had showed up at the motel where Gwen worked, one day, and began to court her despite her all-encompassing lack of interest. Even after two or three lackluster dates, when Gwen had already consigned him to the heap of other disappointed suitors, he was relentless in becoming a part of her life. He had wooed her and charmed her, bringing her expensive presents and cheap mementos. Marcus planned elaborate outings and outlandish surprises, cajoling her into loving him, never displaying his dark side. He never turned on her– until their wedding night.

Marcus wasted no time in explaining the rules of their marriage to Gwen. The new bride didn't pay attention to his words. As a newlywed, she basked in her love for Marcus, and thought his long list of instructions was just one more example of his quirky wit. It didn't take long for her to learn that he was serious.

We uncovered no great insights and made no headway on the reasons for his behavior until we were left with no explanation other than the twisted logic of his deranged mind.

And speaking of Marcus' deranged mind, he called one night.

"Hello."

"Hello, Leo? How the hell are you?"

"Who is this?"

"It's me, Marcus. I need to speak to Gwen. Go get her!"

"I'm not sure she'll want to speak to you."

"Tell her, her husband's on the phone. She'll speak to me, all right."

"I can almost guarantee that if you cop that attitude, she won't."

"I guess you and Dara have had your chance to turn Gwen against me, haven't you? I've told you before, it won't last. Tell Gwen I'm waiting. If she knows what's good for her, she'll talk to me."

"I'll give her the message."

There was a flash of Dara in Gwen's eyes as she took the phone from me. Yes!

"What is it, Marcus?"

"Gwen, baby, how are you?"

"You've heard from the courts, right?"

"Some asshole gave me a subpoena. I told him it was a mistake. My Gwennie wouldn't do that."

"It wasn't a mistake. I'm divorcing you. I want you out of my life. My life and Carrie's."

"But Gwennie, don't say that. I love you so. I couldn't live without you. You know that. And my pretty baby girl. How is she?"

"Fuck you!"

"Don't you talk to me like that. I'm still your husband. I still tell you what to do. Now get your ass out here!"

"I"m through with you and your orders, Marcus. Find someone else to torture. You're never going to see either me or Carrie again."

"You don't really mean that. It's that bastard Leo and your fucking mother trying to take my Gwennie away from me."

"Nice try, Marcus. I stopped being your *Gwennie* when you killed my baby and almost killed me. Now go away. You want to talk, talk to my lawyer. The court will give you his number. Don't ever call here again."

"I'm coming to get you right now. I'll be on the first plane out. We're going away from there– the three of us."

"I've got a restraining order. If you show up anywhere near this place, I'll have you arrested."

Marcus cried and babbled about all the wrongs that the world was doing to him. He couldn't get a job, the Salem police were looking for him to question him about Gwen's beating, he had nowhere to live, no money, and he was drinking heavily. He needed Gwen's comfort. He needed Gwen. Or sometimes he demanded Gwen, ordered her to him. Gwen held the phone away from her ear. After a while, she put it down and left the room.

I was proud of her. It was the first time she had stood up to Marcus. I let Marcus rant on for a few more minutes then picked up the receiver.

"Marcus. Leo. Gwen left. I told you she wouldn't let you Marcus her any more. Go away and leave her alone. It's over. Go away!"

"I'll get you all for this. I'll get you good. Nobody fucks with me."

"This conversation is over. Don't try to contest the divorce or Gwen will press charges. You've lost. For once, take it like a man." I slammed the receiver down on its cradle.

Dara had been listening to the whole thing– when I had answered the phone, what Gwen had said and done, and my closing remarks to Marcus.

"Thank God it's over."

"Is it?."

Again, I was the only one who didn't immediately recover from the encounter with Marcus. Dara had expressed her opinion that it was all over and meant it. Gwen was almost euphoric at the successful outcome of her first confrontation with him. I couldn't shake my sense of foreboding. Marcus was too insane to be thwarted so easily, and I didn't share their complacency. We each went back to our passions.

Gwen read.

Leo painted.

Dara Daraed.

With each passing day, Gwen metamorphosed from her chrysalis. She became more confident, more assertive (it was about time those genes expressed themselves) and she was pushing her horizons further and further back. One evening, she came to us with a new proposal.

"Mom, Leo, I want to write my story."

"What do you mean, *write*? An article, a diary, a book?"

"A book. To help myself and others. I want to look at it all in one piece, and I think other women would want to read it, too."

"But you're just coming out from under Marcus' control. Wouldn't it be too depressing, too painful for you?"

"It's what I want to do."

"Well then, you certainly have my support. What do you think Dara? Ready to design a cover? I'll do anything that I can to help. I'm sure Mo must know someone in the . . ."

"That's just it. I want your help most of all, Leo."

"Sure. What can I do?"

"I want to write it as your story."

"I don't understand."

"Writing it as my own story doesn't make sense.. I wasn't aware of what was going on through most of it, and Mom was a basket case You're the only one who was aware of exactly what was going on. Only your voice could tell it."

"Do you know how long it took me to write notes on my paintings? I'm not a writer."

"I don't want you to write it, I'm going to write it, I just want to use your voice and your memory."

I thought about it for a while, then agreed.

Of course I agreed. There was no reason not to agree. We spent a lot of time together, after that, in my studio. While I painted, Gwen wrote her (my?) story on the word processor and, from time to time, asked me to fill in the details of events that occurred away from the main, Marcus and Gwen, action.

Of course I agreed. There was no reason not to. And, in recounting the details, I got a sharper perspective of the whole picture for myself.

Of course I agreed. There was no reason not to.

Until I lived the last chapter.

Chapter 35

The book progressed at an erratic pace. Sometimes the story told itself, spilling out in whole chapters, while at other times, the words settled unwillingly onto the page. But Gwen slogged through the tough spots– usually the descriptions of Marcus' treatment of her as seen through my eyes. Sometimes, I caused the slowdowns when we got to parts where it was difficult for me to recount the details of my intimate relations with her mother, or to license the transcription of my inner thoughts for all the world to see.

Eventually, and especially as Gwen's enthusiasm for her work grew, I became more comfortable, and was able to lose myself in my own work, as I casually, and almost unconsciously, related my disgust and horror over Gwen's predicament and my tumultuous separation from Dara. By the third week, the book became just a story, and the characters in the story just did what they did.

The dynamics of our family changed, too. With subtlety at first, and then, in greater measures as Gwen's book progressed. The first was a change in Gwen's relationship with Carrie. Gwen, at last, acted like she was Carrie's mother. Before coming to the studio to write, she spent the first two hours of every day with Carrie Then, after dinner, it was Gwen who read to Carrie until her bedtime.

My relationship with Dara had always been intense, but never all consuming because of the way we both felt about our work. Thus, Dara and I didn't always spend a lot of time together– we were more like each other's reward at the end of a long day, or even a hectic week. Not until recently did we sleep together every night ,and therefore, saw each other every day.

That hadn't changed, but now I was spending six to eight hours of every day with Gwen. I had never spent that much time alone with anyone except my brother Zach when we were children. A year ago, I had been summarily dismissed from Gwen's life. Now, I was collaborating on a book about that life, spending most of my day with her.

Our relationship was rapidly changing from surrogate father/daughter, to colleagues, to friends. Our friendship developed faster than Gwen and Dara's friendship. However, in another way, it hastened the Dara-Gwen friendship. Now, evenings were more like three friends getting together than a family.

This, in turn, dissipated the last outposts of stress, enhancing my relationship with Dara. We were all riding high.

The only troublesome spot in our lives were the increasingly frequent phone calls from Marcus. If Dara or I answered the phone, we'd hear heavy breathing for a few seconds followed by a click. When Gwen picked up the phone, Marcus either begged or ordered her to his side. Gwen always hung up before Marcus had finished his first sentence. Her dismissal infuriated him, prompting even more calls.

We decided against getting an unlisted number because hearing from Marcus was more reassuring than not knowing if he might, unexpectedly, turn up. Gwen was completely against an unlisted number. She refused to be manipulated by Marcus ever again, even by something as trivial as changing her phone number.

After six weeks, Marcus abruptly stopped calling. His motives were unclear. We knew we couldn't count on sane thinking from Marcus– like, *She's not listening to me, why should I continue to bother calling?–* so there would have to be another, less rational, reason. All we knew was that we hadn't heard the last of him.

In a way, we were wrong.

Marcus never did call again, but a few weeks later, Dara received a call at work from Marcus' father. Richard Davis had been called by the Mexican authorities who reported that his son, Marcus, had committed suicide. They were holding his body, awaiting instructions on its disposal. Mr. Davis wondered whether Gwen wanted to make funeral arrangements or have his parents do it. Dara took it upon herself to answer for Gwen, telling Marcus' father to make the plans himself. She called me at the studio to let me know.

"Here, why don't you tell Gwen yourself?"

"Do you think I should? Over the phone?"

"I think she'd want you to. Plus, she's hearing all this."

"Well, tell her I'll be right there. I'd rather tell her in person." She hung up.

"That was Dara."

"Duh."

"Anyway, she has some news about Marcus that she wants to tell you in person. She'll be right here."

"She could have saved herself the trip. I'm not interested in news about Marcus."

"She's on her way. You can tell her that when she gets here."

Dara didn't give Gwen a chance not to listen to her story. There wasn't much to tell and she blurted it out in one piece as soon as she came through the door. Gwen's reaction was inscrutable.

Her tone and her expression never changed. She didn't ask Dara any questions, although, even if she had, there weren't any details available. Still, she was almost too serene– like she was in a state of shock that might crumble at any moment. But she didn't. She just didn't.

The topic of conversation over the next few days, while we waited for word from the Davises, was what Gwen should do about the funeral. Go? Not go? Send flowers? Write a note? Ignore the whole thing?

Dara wanted to ignore the whole thing. She had personally suffered ever since Marcus had come into our lives, and wanted to be rid of Marcus forever. Dara didn't need closure, she had already closed. Dara hated Marcus for what he had done to Gwen more than for what pain he had caused her, and she didn't want Gwen to *validate his pathetic little existence* with her presence at his funeral. She would have preferred to leave Marcus to rot in Mexico, and not have a funeral at all.

I wanted to go, mainly for myself, for the answers to the many lingering questions I needed to understand. I couldn't do what Dara had done. I couldn't will myself to put Marcus out of my mind. Meeting Marcus' parents would help. They would have the answer to some of my questions. If I had to paint Marcus' portrait, it would have been one dimensional. Marcus was a caricature, a cliche, an indelible question mark. I was totally devoid of insight concerning him. And yet, he was my daughter's husband and my granddaughter's father. It wasn't right that he should die and still remain a cipher.

Gwen vacillated from day to day, from hour to hour. She had grown from a woman who was totally enthralled, in both senses, by Marcus, to one who was free from his control– a clear thinking, self-motivated young woman who'd left her life with Marcus behind as she came into her own. She didn't need to go to the funeral.

But she shared my curiosity about Marcus, and wanted to finally meet Marcus' parents, if for no other reason than to find out why she hadn't been allowed to meet them in the past. They were Carrie's grandparents, after all, and Gwen had to decide if they belonged in Carrie's life. Just a few days before, Gwen had wanted Marcus erased from their past. Marcus, his family, and his name. Now that he was dead, she wasn't quite as sure about his parents.

We waited for three days before Mr. Davis called back– Marcus' body would arrive from Mexico on Friday morning and the funeral would be on Sunday morning in accordance with Jewish laws which did not allow Sabbath burials. Dara took down the pertinent information along with directions to the funeral parlor, but did not commit to Gwen's attendance. She told Mr. Davis to proceed as planned. If Gwen decided to come, she would be there.

Gwen waffled over her decision until Saturday night. Sometimes, she wasn't going to go at all. At other times, she would go alone. Still other times, she begged Dara and me to go with her for support. We each continued to give our own opinions, which only added to her confusion. In the end, Gwen decided that if she didn't go, she might regret it later. If she went, she had nothing to lose and she'd forestall future self-recrimination. We went, all of us.

And came close to missing the funeral. The traffic was heavier than we had anticipated, and we got lost because Dara had incompletely scrawled the directions, not expecting to need them. Dara had decided for Gwen, forgetting that Gwen was changed– more capable of making her own decisions, and more willing to proceed counter to Dara's opinion. We arrived just as the service was about to begin, having missed the pre-funeral family grief-sharing.

Gwen identified herself to one of the funeral directors at the back of the chapel, and he directed us to reserved seats in the first row. We walked down the aisle.

Marcus' parents were already seated in the first row across the aisle from our seats. A young woman was walking down the aisle about fifteen feet in front of us, partially obscuring my view of the Davises whose backs were turned to us, anyway. The young woman greeted them as she approached.

I had been walking down the aisle between Gwen and Dara, holding hands with both of them. My hands slid up to their shoulders for support as my knees buckled. I gasped. The blood drained out of my brain and my heart pounded at a breakaway speed.

I fell to my knees, disoriented.

I stared at Marcus' mother.

Carole Davis.

Carrie's namesake. Carole.

Everything was suddenly clear. Crystal clear. Too clear. My stomach turned, and I was sickened, almost vomited. I understood.

Marcus' mother.

Carole Davis.

The former Carole Sylvia Birmbaum.

Sylvie!

Epilogue
Sylvie's Version

Before either Dara or Gwen could do anything, Sylvie was kneeling at my side, frantic. Despite my disoriented state, I could see that her eyes were huge and round and that she, too, was ashen.

"Leo, I swear, I didn't know. How could I know? Who would have thought . . . ?"

"Leo, are you okay?" (Dara)

"What's going on?" (Gwen)

"Mrs. Davis, could you give him some room? I don't know either, Gwen. Let's make sure Leo is okay, first."

My mind was slowly recovering from the shock of instantaneous revelation. I knew and understood– not every detail, but enough. My body was taking control of itself, and though still woozy, I climbed to my feet using a seat edge for support.

"Dara, meet Sylvie." I gestured from one to the other. Now Dara looked like Sylvie and me. Although at the time, she didn't quite grasp why, she sensed the demons in the wings.

"Who's Sylvie?"

"Marcus' mother and my first wife."

Rather than paling, Gwen just quizzically looked at us both. She hadn't made the connection of anything with anything, but Dara's face, although still puzzled, showed she understood that the Marcus-Sylvie connection was at the root of everything. After that, Marcus' funeral was secondary to the true action.

First, everyone got introduced to everyone else: The Davises, Mr. & Mrs.; the Harringtons, mother and daughter– or was Gwen still a Davis? and Leo Schultz, Mr. and ex-Mrs., and sort-of-Mrs.

Somewhere in between the real events, a funeral service was held. Contrary to our original plan, we stayed for the actual burial. Everyone, except the rabbi tried to rush through the rituals so we could get down to the important activity of the day– talking privately. After interminable hours of shaking hands and nodding to strangers, we finally gathered at Sylvie's home to have our discussion.

With Sylvie and Richard's help, as well as Marcus' sister, Brianna– but. more importantly, with papers eventually recovered from Mexico, we pieced together the whole sick and sickening story.

Marcus' family were in agreement that Marcus had always been *different*, only the degree of difference varied– from father, *he was always a loner*; to mother, *I sensed he was troubled from the time he was a child, and he got worse all the time*; to his sister, *he was a fucking whacko*.

As he grew older, his few friendships disappeared, and he became more bitter and out of synch with his world. He started reading ultra-right wing magazines and, although both his parents were Jewish, neo-Nazi propaganda. As a teenager, he made a futile attempt at mainstreaming when he became interested in sex. Unfortunately for him, for his family, for Gwen and for me, he was rejected by every girl he approached. The disappointments turned into a hatred of all women, but a hatred of his mother most of all.

He blamed Sylvie for everything that happened to him and for all his failures. Rather than the docile and humble Madonna he required, Sylvie was a brassy, self-indulgent and outwardly sexy woman. And she had come to her marriage as a non-virgin and a divorcee. Used goods. Violated.

As Marcus' sickness grew, he demanded that Sylvie apologize for her life, that she become contrite in the face of Marcus' righteousness. She laughed at him and ignored him, feeding his misogynous wrath and mocking his holier-than-thou attitude.

When he became more incensed and belligerent at home, he was sent for therapy, but refused to go regularly. He berated his father for being subservient, and his mother for being a whore and an egoist. His mental health deteriorated to such a large extent that when he went away to college, his parents asked him not to return home until he'd had significant therapy.

Marcus was impotent to do anything to punish them. They were paying for his school, and Sylvie, although a harlot, *was* his mother. In his warped interpretation of his new morality, he was obligated to honor and respect her because she was his mother, even though he loathed her as a woman. His father was beneath his contempt.

Then he made a psychotic leap of reasoning.

Since Sylvie was the source of all his problems, and her culpability was directly related to her status as an unrepentant fallen woman, it followed, then, that the man who had felled her was the true cause, the root cause, of it all. The man who had deflowered Sylvie, whoever that was, certainly no one I knew, and the man who had divorced her (this one I knew) was the real culprit. To Marcus, who was horrified that his mother had sex with any other man, and couldn't even fathom the possibility that there had been more than one, the deflowerer and the divorcer were one and the same. He rolled all of his hatred into hatred for one man: Leo Shultz, Satan incarnate.

Me. Leo. Whom I like to think of as lovable Leo. I was the ultimate object of Marcus' loathing and depravity. And he owed me no allegiance, no consideration. He could hate me guiltlessly and sanctimoniously, and with the full measure of his psychotic enmity. He would have his revenge. He plotted to make me pay for his sorry life.

And that became the GRAND PLAN of Marcus Davis– the systematic destruction of everything Leo Schultz held dear, followed by my ultimate financial ruin. First Gwen. Then Dara. Then my reputation. Then my fortune. It was all revealed in a journal he kept in meticulous detail to chart his delusions.

But his plan failed for many reasons. Marcus fought for revenge while we struggled for our lives. Marcus was acting alone while we, from time to time at least, had each other. Marcus was profoundly psychotic while we were all just deeply neurotic.

His plan failed, he was wanted by the Salem police for questioning about Gwen's beating, and he was jobless, without prospect, and penniless. He retreated to an informal beach commune in Baja where many American expatriates lived. These people were there because they pursued alternative lifestyles, and were there to escape family pressures, U.S. laws, and the occasional felony conviction. They used drugs and advocated sexual freedom and experimentation. Marcus' ultra-moral stance soon made him a pariah among pariahs. When he was served with divorce papers from Gwen, and discovered his hold on her had dissolved, he was finished. And he knew it. And for once, he acted appropriately.

That was the fruit of his vengeful, twisted mind.

Epilogue
Dara's Version

I was sprawled on the floor. When I tried to look up at Dara to tell her I was okay, Sylvie was already standing over me, her grimacing lips stretched tautly over her teeth exposed behind a vicious leer.

"Leo, you bastard. How dare you come here?"

I struggled to my feet and gestured from Dara to Sylvie. It was all suddenly so painfully clear to me. Marcus, Sylvie. Marcus and Sylvie. Marcus and Gwen. And at the bottom of it all, Sylvie. Years of only half-remembered hate bubbled up behind my eyes, filling my consciousness. I tasted the bitter taste of Sylvie's anima once again. My life had happy times and bad times– the bad times all centered around Sylvie.

"Dara, meet Sylvie. Sylvie, Dara."

Dara hadn't quite put it together yet, but she understood the essence of what she was witnessing. Her eyes, glued now on Sylvie, grew menacing– volcanic combustion ready to melt Sylvie with their molten flow. Gwen looked at the three of us with a confused look on her face.

"What's going on?"

I was regaining my composure. Still leaning on the chapel bench, I half turned to Gwen.

"Marcus' mother, as bizarre as it may seem, is my ex-wife."

Gwen remained confused.

"I don't think Marcus just happened upon you, I think he came looking for you as part of some grotesque plan. And I'm sure, somehow, that Marcus' mother is at the center of it all."

"Leo, I swear, I had nothing to do with anything that Marcus might have done."

"Save it, Sylvie."

"What are you saying? What are you accusing me of?"

"I don't know yet, but I'll figure it out."

"Damn you, Leo. Whatever he was, I lost my son. Damn your smugness and damn your superiority."

Sylvie was in my face and pounding on my chest. Dara caught Sylvie's arm in mid-pummel and spun her around. Dara became the mother tiger defending her daughter, through my proxy, against the venomous snake. Her look brooked no counteroffensive. She pushed Sylvie into retreat with her eyes.

"Don't. It wouldn't be wise."

That's all Dara needed to say. Sylvie backed off.

Somehow, a funeral service was performed. We stayed for the actual burial so that we could have time alone with Sylvie and her husband. As unsavory as that prospect seemed, we wanted the information we had come for in the first place.

Richard and Sylvie each had their own perspective, and didn't add much to what we already knew. We learned the most from Marcus' sister and, then, from Marcus' journal, which was eventually recovered from Mexico.

Marcus' sister had been telling her parents that Marcus was crazy from the time they were children. Young Marcus had little to do with other children– he didn't play any sports, and he only joined in with the other kids when they were doing something mean or cruel. Mostly, he brooded. Brianna was afraid to be alone with Marcus because he was downright sadistic and enjoyed tormenting her and her friends. Other children's parents wouldn't let them come to the Davis' to play. Richard and Sylvie minimized the situation, attributing Brianna's warnings to sibling rivalry.

At best, Sylvie had been a disinterested mother. She had failed herself when she had left me. Richard Davis was a successful businessman and a rich man, but he wasn't famous like Leo Schultz. Even though Sylvie loved Richard in her way, and more than she'd ever loved me, Leo was so much more important than Richard, and could have provided Sylvie with the things she wanted most.

Sylvie would have made my importance work for her. She would have been the queen of Radical Chic, the spokeswoman of the New York Art scene. Famous people would seek her friendship just to have their names linked with hers. But she'd thrown away her chance 'to matter' by making certain suppositions and certain predictions, by overestimating the brightness of her constellation in my firmament. She misjudged my ability to get out from under her dominion because I had been such a needy puppy dog when we first met.

My former wife hadn't guessed the proper order of my priorities assuming, because my painting was just a means to her, that my passion for her would supercede my passion to paint. If she had spent any time at all trying to get to know her husband, she would have realized that my passion for my work defined me. Even a cursory look would have told her that.

Sylvie had been too busy with her own plans to look. Not taking my values into account, she assumed I would hang onto any relationship she would allow, and be thankful for it.. She hadn't anticipated my ability to shut myself off inside my work, and not care what became of Sylvie.

Her final bad decision was precipitated by Richard's arrival on the scene. He was handsome and rich, and liked to party. Richard was deeply in love with Sylvie and told her that if she married him, she could do whatever she wanted. How could she resist?

They married and had two children right away. Sylvie took up golf and tennis, and ran charity balls. Their suburban community was not a big enough stage for Sylvie. Being the darling of Westchester's jet set didn't satisfy her needs.

When she, frequently, lost patience with her children, she reminded them of what she had given up to be their mother. In fact, she reminded everyone who would listen of what she had given up as Mrs. Leo Schultz to become Mrs. Richard Davis. By the time her new marriage was four-years-old, she had convinced herself of the attention and admiration she would have achieved if only she'd held onto Leo, and that she had been unjustly robbed of her true destiny. None of it was her fault because she was, after all, Sylvie. The blame must lie with me.

Brianna, the younger of the two children, recognized, almost from birth, that there would be no succor from Sylvie, so no future in pursuing her mother's affection. She allied herself with her father from the start, limiting her relationship with her mother to passing greetings punctuated with occasional instructions. No love, no warmth. As far as she was concerned, her mother was a bitter, selfish bitch– a non-being in the girl's life.

The story was different for Marcus. As a little boy, he followed his mother around everywhere, hoping for tidbits of attention and small signs of love. He yearned for his emotionally absent mother, and never got enough from her to satisfy hid needs. Sylvie was always too preoccupied with her own suffered fate. Her abandonment affected him in a deep, disturbing way.

Marcus went from abject devotion, to unrequited love, to loathing. Loathing for his unresponsive mother and loathing for the ultimate cause of her preoccupation. He became engorged with his hatred of a man he had never met, a man unaware of Marcus' existence. Me.

Now Carole Davis, Sylvie made no secret of blaming her dissatisfied life on me for casting her off. Me, for not appreciating the gift of herself that she had bestowed upon me. Me, for cutting her off from a life of fame and fortune, the life she was meant to have.

Mother gave birth to son. Her hatred was Marcus' hatred, but the hatred became more twisted as it passed through him. I was the devil, the repository of all that was wrong in his universe, and I needed to be defeated to restore his mother's love. As his plan took root, his soul began to putrefy and his bloated abhorrence threatened to explode. Marcus plummeted into psychosis.

You know the plan, you've read all the details, the story is hardly original– Marcus was neither bright nor imaginative. The people around Marcus make this story unique– Gwen and Dara and me. Especially, I think, me.

I have thought of myself as Gwen's father for a long time. I love Gwen and would do anything for her. And I love her mother more than, or certainly as much as, any man has ever loved a woman. I am my painting, but aside from my painting, I am also my family.

Dara and Gwen, and Carrie. At this point, there is no separation between who I am, and who I am as a husband and a father

But I'd missed the early bonding with Gwen, and now that I have experienced infancy with Carrie, I realize that it is a big thing. Do I love Gwen because she is a part of me, or do I love her because she is a part of Dara who, in turn, is a part of me? Do I love her as Dara's daughter or as my daughter?

Conversely, I have no attachments to Marcus. I was married to his mother once, but that was, as they say, long ago and far away. Marcus was conceived long after I stopped having sex with Sylvie. And yet, my mere existence was the main shaping tool of Marcus' life. My impact on his mother's relationship with him was the thing that caused him to be who he was, to think as he did, to act as he'd acted. Though Marcus didn't have a single strand of my DNA in him, isn't he, in a larger sense, my doing?

Isn't he my son?

Epilogue
Gwen's Version

The things I've learned from writing this book! The things I've learned about myself and Marcus and Dara. The things I've learned about Sylvie, whom I never knew at all. And Leo? Well, I've always known everything there is to know about Leo.

It's been several years, now, since I last saw Marcus. That last time replays in my mind over and over like a tune you can't stop humming. Marcus had been drinking, which always made him act crazier than usual. He was bound to get angry at me no matter what I did, so I tried to fade into the walls and be inconspicuous. But we lived in a one-room trailer and there was no place for me to go.

Inevitably, he got angry because I *was ignoring him.* He berated me for everything that I'd ever done to annoy him. Nothing I did helped. If I protested his words, he got angrier. If I did nothing, he got angrier. If I tried to flee, he got angrier.

There was a pot of soup boiling on the stove. He flung it at me, scalding my chest and arms. His fury intensified as he beat me with his fists and then kicked me when I was on the floor. In between, he had sex with me. Technically, I guess, it was rape. I didn't regain full consciousness for days.

I haven't been around any men since Marcus. Except, of course, Leo. Dara assumes that I am afraid of all men, and afraid that I am unable to face a new relationship for fear that it will turn out like my marriage. That's not it, not it at all. The real reason is very different.

I love Marcus.

I know I'm not supposed to love him, not even supposed to think about loving him. Or about Marcus himself– I'm supposed to be *over him*, recovered from him. I don't want to be over him, I want him with me always. I love Marcus and, despite what everyone tells me, I know that Marcus loved me.

I've played along with my mother's game, but it was all a charade to me. I had to be with her. I had to be here even though she pretends that she'd given me a choice, that I could have made it on my own. She forgets that she is the one who created me– created me to do her bidding.

Being here and watching her watch me was too much to bear, so I retreated into books. That made her happier and further diluted her ever-present disapproval. Nothing except my total renunciation of Marcus would satisfy her. I gave her what she wanted with my words. I kept Marcus just for me– in my heart.

No one would expect a woman to give up on her husband if he had a heart disease, or epilepsy, or even AIDS. No one would condone giving up on a husband who was afraid of heights or even one who had fugue states. Well, Marcus had a sickness just as real as any of those others. Do I abandon the very memory of him because he was sick? That's not something I would teach Carrie. Dara thinks, and is very proud of herself for it, that she has taught me this lesson well.

Dara, Dara, Dara, Dara. Dara my mother. Dara my creator. Dara my teacher. Dara my undoing.

And what made Marcus the way he was? Was it all genetic, totally beyond anyone's control, passed down by an entire lineage of crazed ancestors? Would Marcus be the same person if his father had given him the attention he'd lavished on Brianna? What if Sylvie had been a real mother? Would Marcus have been allowed to drift further and further into chaos?

Perhaps Richard and Sylvie were well-meaning parents whose motives and actions were distorted by the chemically imbalanced mind of their son. Perhaps Marcus was possessed by the devil, or driven to insanity by cosmic injustices only his genius comprehended. Whatever caused his dysfunction altered his perceptions and reshaped him into who he was.

In his mind, he was Marcus, a child with the bad luck to have Sylvie as his mother. Once he'd been expelled from her body, he was exiled from her mind and from her life. She was so concerned with Sylvie that she had no time left to consider Marcus. All he ever felt from Sylvie were neglect and ridicule– and she was the parent he identified with most.

Whatever the real relationship between Marcus and his parents, and whatever caused his mental disease, these were his perceptions and were the basis of his memory– to him they were real. They were what he remembered and what caused him to act the way he did. So let's vilify Marcus and celebrate his suicide. Let's erase his name from our minds and expunge his life from our memories. Society is much better off without him. Certainly Gwen back-to-Harrington is.

Dara wasn't Sylvie. Not to me and not to Leo. Her controlling micro management style of child raising could never be mistaken for neglect. Sometimes I prayed for neglect. Everyone said my mother was self-assured. To me, she was haughty and arrogant. While she never verbally ridiculed me, she always made me feel that I could never be the woman she was– her eyes, those damn eyes that Leo loves so much, reflected her silent disappointment.

It wasn't as if this all-knowing, never to be questioned motherhood arose from the loftiest experiences and after arduous study of parenting. My dear mother stumbled into maternity during a time of her life she would rather forget.

As an adolescent, I desperately needed to know my father's identity. I looked at passing strangers' faces hoping to see a glint of recognition in some man's eyes. I didn't know about my mother's past at the time, of course, and that she had no more idea who my father was than I did. Dara was no help, so I got more and more frustrated with my fatherlessness.

Reality failed me, so I turned to fantasy. If I couldn't know my own father, I would invent a perfect surrogate who would love me without limit, and rescue me from any bad situation. Unquestioning and nonjudgmental, he would suppress his own needs to respond to mine.

Leo Schultz often seems too good to be true. He is. Leo doesn't exist, never existed, and will never exist outside of my mind and the pages of this book. Exiled from my monstrous mother, and sequestered by my abusive husband, I invented my rescuer from a little girl's father-fantasies and a young woman's unrequited needs.

He would love my mother, too. They would share an all-encompassing love that let each other be who they were. He would be charming and rich and very famous. To suit my mother, he would have something to do with Art, and be mellow and understanding. My father-ideal would serve as a great counterbalance to my mother's personality.

This Leo Schultz would be all things to me. My father. My mother's lover. My own pure and chaste knight errant. My confidant and my collaborator. My best friend. He would be more perfect than any real man could. And mine, all mine, because he would only exist inside me.

No wonder Marcus gravitated toward me— we were both fantasizers. He had to create a better mother from his imagination because his flesh and blood mother was of no use.

I became his fantasy. I was, at once, his wife and his mother. I was his virgin and his slave girl, satisfying his lust while striving to attain a holy state. Predestined for failure, I could only fail. No one can compete with fantasy.

Dara needed a fantasy too. She was too headstrong and controlling to attract the sort of man she wanted— a man who was successful and committed to his work, a man who would love her despite her numerous neuroses, and no matter how she treated him during her fits of self-doubt. A man who completed her and whom she completed. Maybe everyone needs a fantasy of one kind or another to stave off the cruelties of reality.

Sylvie was totally dissatisfied with her life, with what she had let herself become. She had finished college with great career plans and abandoned them for the rich and attractive Richard Davis. She couldn't accept that she had wittingly chosen money over fulfillment. She created her own Leo, someone on whom to heap the blame.

Marcus never had a chance. I never had a chance. In the end, Marcus and I as a couple never had a chance. Maybe Carrie will have a chance. Maybe.

This is my story. It 's the story of my love for two men– one real, but imperfect and dead; and the other a product of my unfilled needs. It 's the story of several women– one whom I hate for destroying the man I love, and one whom I adore because she is the fruit of that love. And of my mother whom I both hate and love. Whom I both fear and pity. This is the story of a dull gray moth who wished she had been born a butterfly, and had to imagine the colors for herself.

About the Author

Jack Chalfin was born in Brooklyn, N.Y., received an undergraduate degree in philosophy from Hobart College, and a medical degree from the State University of New York. Jack began a fulltime career in fiction writing, a lifelong passion, after more than twenty years as an ophthalmologist, while recovering from a kidney/pancreas organ transplant. He is the author of several novels, as well as short stories, poetry, and numerous scientific articles. At the age of fifteen, Jack wrote a coming-of-age novel called Memoirs of A Moth, which was so bad that the only salvageable part was the title.

The author has lived in New York, Boston, Chicago, Geneva, Barcelona, and London before moving to Cape Cod. Now that his son, Max, has gone off to college, he continues to live on Cape Cod with his wife, Claire, and his dog.

Printed in the United States
31496LVS00005B/55-60